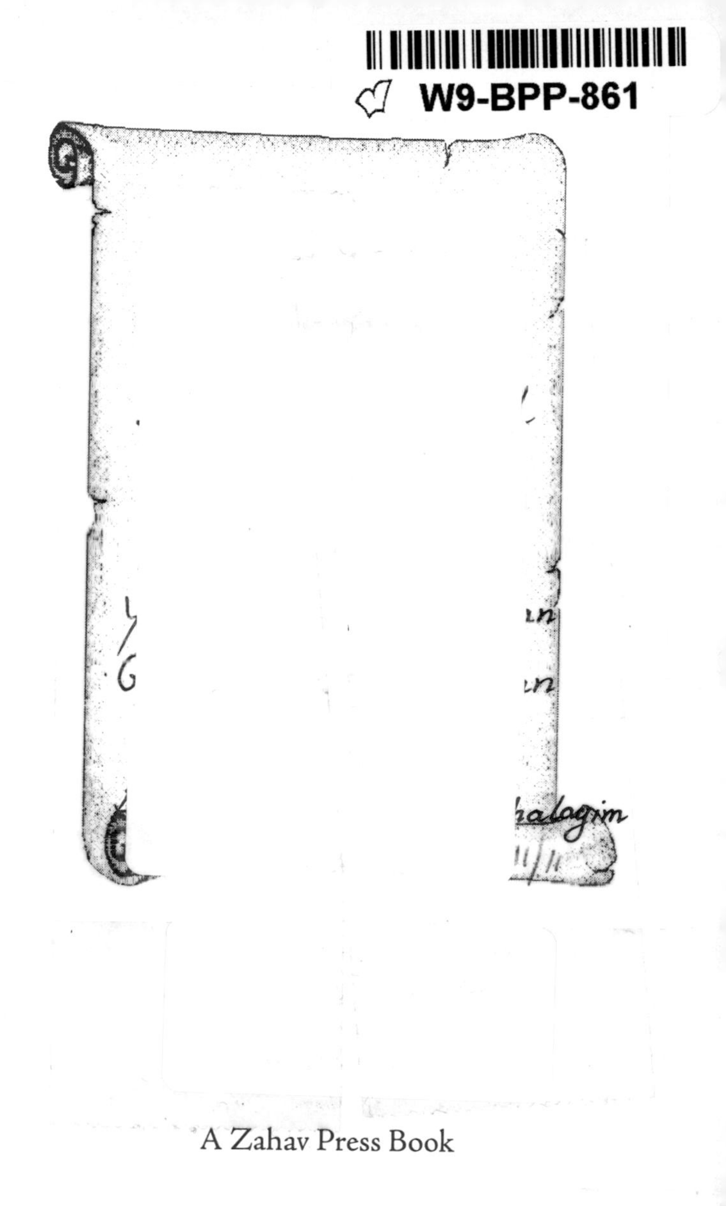

A Zahav Press Book

First published 2010

ISBN 978-1-56871-536-0

Published and distributed by:
Zahav Press
5809 16th Avenue
Brooklyn, NY 11204
E-mail: info@zahavpress.com
www.zahavpress.com

Acknowledgments

THANK YOU TO MY KIND first readers who offered excellent insights and advice for improvement, often on twenty-four hours' notice: Lisa Biggar, Jane Ackerman, Dishy Shiffman, Sara Jaffe, and my beloved husband, Stephen Jaffe.

A special thank-you to my daughter, Sara, who, upon reading my manuscript, made an important observation. Where I had written a line for one of my characters: "I did it, *baruch Hashem*!" she pointed out that the sentence should read, "*Baruch Hashem,* I did it!" Her lesson reverberates for me to this day.

A special acknowledgment belongs with my husband, Stephen, who tolerated the sometimes-transparent parallels between this script and our own life together. I promised him — only a portion of this book is autobiographical. The rest is complete fiction. It is up to you, dear readers, to figure out which part is fiction.

Thank you to *Mishpacha* magazine, where I am privileged to be a regular writer, and my good friend Yitta Halberstam, who led me to *Mishpacha* in the first place. It was my work with *Mishpacha* that led me, in a circuitous way, to meet the editors of this project.

Thank you to the talented and committed editors at Zahav Press for believing in me and allowing me this opportunity. May this be the first of many!

Thank you to the Yeshiva at IDT, where I'm kept on my toes as an English professor through the many students who have improved my writing by asking questions and demanding the best from me. Thanks also for the laughter. You make it fun to go to work. I don't plan on making an English composition assignment out of this book...but you never know.

To my children, Sara, Elana, and Elijah: you are what shapes my life and gives it meaning.

To my Creator: May I always be a *kiddush Hashem,* in Your eyes and in the eyes of others. Thank you.

Azriela Jaffe

One

Devoiry wiped her messy hands on her much-used apron and stared ruefully at her latest attempt to transform a simple tortilla and cheese dish into kosher gourmet extraordinaire. "Kosher gourmet in thirty minutes or less" — that's my tagline. Maybe it should be "Kosher but disappointing, try take-out instead."

Devoiry's ego had been seriously bruised lately since finding out from her publisher that her new gourmet cookbook, *Kosher Gourmet in Less Time Than It Takes to Order Out,* even with all of the publisher's Chanukah promotions, had sold a whopping — drum roll, please — 534 copies, and the publisher warned that at least one-third of them would be returned, a common occurrence amongst cookbook aficionados who buy a new cookbook, scan it for a few favorite recipes, and then return it. *Mr. Weiss,* she thought to herself, *you think I'm doing this big chesed by having you over week after week for dinner, but you have no idea how good it is to hear you rave about my cooking. Honestly, I should pay you as my therapist!* Jacob Weiss, widowed from her mom's best friend, Tzipporah, a little over a year ago, was a regular Tuesday evening guest of the Rosenberg family. He was due for dinner in less than two hours and she had no idea what she was going to feed him.

Devoiry glanced at the wall clock and startled at the time: 4:50 p.m. The kids would be rushing off the school bus any minute, starting with her baby, third-grader Naftali, arriving on the boys' elementary school bus at 5, followed by middle-schoolers Bracha, just turned 14, and Malka, 10, almost 11, at 5:15, who were lucky enough to be able to walk home from the small girls' middle-school recently built just down the block from their home. At least she had a bit more time to prepare dinner for Mordy, her six-foot-tall, skinny-as-a-beanpole high-schooler, who didn't get home till 9-10 p.m. each night, depending on night *seder*. He was always ravenous from his one-hour bus trip from the boys' high school yeshivah slightly out of town, and his yeshivah diet of largely, decidedly nongourmet food did nothing to put meat on his bones. Fattening up Mordy was one of her daily obsessions.

Now what should I do about dinner? Devoiry fretted. Adding jalapenos and feta cheese to this dish was a bad idea, and the outcome would be inedible to anyone who had decent taste buds. *I'm usually very careful about ba'al tashchis, but this dish can hardly be considered food anymore.*

With a glance at the clock, Devoiry sprung into action. She plugged in her dependable sandwich maker to prewarm, grabbed a loaf of the kids' favorite potato bread out of the freezer (*oy, this bread has no nutrients or fiber. And it's so tasteless!*), and to make herself feel better about at least serving her kids a vegetable, grabbed her tomato knife and swiftly sliced up a handful of tomatoes to dress up the sandwiches.

"Come on, come on, warm up already," she urged the machine, waiting impatiently for the red light to turn green.

The front door flew open and a frigid gust of air from the Lancaster, Pennsylvania, winter, accompanied Naftali as he rushed into the marble-tiled foyer, flung his backpack into the corner, kicked off his winter boots, and shouted, "Mommy, I got 104 on the spelling test, top mark in the class!"

"Fabulous!" Devoiry called out to him. "I'm so proud of you. I know how hard you studied for that test. Mommy is making you a grilled cheese sandwich. Come wash your hands and when it's ready we'll make *hamotzi*."

The light turned green, and in ten seconds flat, faster than the time it took Naftali to cross the large expanse of their dining room, his grilled cheese was sizzling in the machine. *Whew, saved again by my new best friend, the sandwich maker, ready for dinner emergencies in less than five minutes.*

Naftali wiggled his nose. "Mommy, what's that smell? It smells like...ewww...something strange!"

Devoiry wondered if any of her kids would acquire her appreciation for gourmet food. Certainly not Tully, who much preferred processed "pretend cheese" to real cheese any day of the week.

"Silly, that's feta cheese you're smelling. It's yummy, very expensive, and gourmet. Mommy is making a new recipe!"

Naftali rolled his eyes and grimaced. "Not again, Mommy. Are you going to make me eat it?"

Ouch. Devoiry opened up the sandwich maker to put Naftali's sandwich in. A couple of minutes, dinner, voilà. Lesson learned — don't put feta cheese into tortillas.

Naftali hurried to the sink to wash his hands, stretching his small frame to reach the faucet. "Hmm, smells delish, Mom. Thanks for making me my fave. Is Mr. Weiss coming tonight for dinner?"

"Yes, at his usual time, 7 p.m., like always."

"Mom, why don't you let him eat something normal, like a grilled cheese, instead of feeding him weird food? It's bad enough his wife died. You have to make him eat icky stuff, too?"

Devoiry tousled Naftali's hair and kissed the top of his head. Since she stood at only five feet two, it wouldn't be long before he shot up to her height and beyond. *Always with a sense of humor, this one. I wish it were contagious and your sister Malka would catch it.*

The sandwich maker light turned green again, and Devoiry removed the glistening hot, gooey sandwich with a spatula and placed it in front of Naftali, who was eagerly awaiting dinner on the barstool at the island. "Tully, this one has your name on it!" His eyes lit up and he ran back to the kitchen sink, mumbled his *berachos* as fast as he could, and then pounced on the sandwich as if it were his favorite candy bar.

The door opened, and Malka and Bracha breezed in, arguing in heated voices.

"Stop blaming me — it's not my fault! Why are you getting on my case?" screamed Bracha.

"Because you could have helped me, but you didn't, because you care more about talking with your friends on the phone every night than you do about me!" retorted Malka.

Devoiry groaned as she watched Malka stomp upstairs to her room in her dirty boots, with no regard for the footprints she left on the beige carpeting.

"Malka Esther, you come down here right now and take off those boots! It's wintertime. You know the rules."

But Malka was long gone. *Probably flung over her bed and sobbing into her pillow as usual, with her boots still on, getting dirt and snow all over her bed.* Devoiry looked quizzically at Bracha. "What are you two arguing about now?"

Bracha flung her black, heavy winter parka over the couch and shook her brown, ponytail-length hair out of its ponytail holder. "Mom, Malka has herself all worked up because she failed her science test, and she's blaming me!"

"How so?" asked Devoiry.

Bracha expelled a lungful of air. "She says that 'cause I've had the same teacher before, and I'm smarter than she is, I should help her study more so she won't fail her next test. Give me a break! What am I, her keeper? It's not my fault that she failed the test!"

Bracha marched into the kitchen looking for dinner. Devoiry didn't know what to do next, rush to comfort Malka, or scold Bracha for her outburst.

Devoiry followed Bracha, grabbing the clutter that had been flung in her path and trying to place it into some semblance of order as she walked. "I'm sorry, Bracha. It's not your fault. Malka is, well, you know, uptight about school, and it's hard for her, especially now with her tics. You know how embarrassed she is. She tries so hard..."

You can't see how much pain Malka is in, because for you, it all comes easily. Can't you have some rachmanus on your sister?

"Bracha, listen," she said firmly. "Whatever you think about helping Malka with her schoolwork, in this house, we don't put people down. You know that."

"Mommy, I think that smelly cheese you always buy is terrible!" Naftali called out, his mouth dripping with gooey American cheese.

"Okay, Tully, we know how you feel about feta cheese. Now, Bracha, grilled Muenster with tomatoes?"

Bracha smirked. "Blew another recipe again, Mommy? What was it this time?"

"Maybe I'm just thinking about how much you all look forward to grilled cheese sandwiches!"

Bracha's edginess softened and she broke out in a wide grin, revealing her picture-perfect smile, courtesy of the orthodontist responsible for straightening most of the Jewish smiles in Lancaster.

"Mommy, you can't fool me. Mr. Weiss is coming to dinner tonight and you'd *never* serve him grilled cheese. That's too *normal*. He always gets something *phenomenal* instead."

Devoiry flinched. *Can't get anything past this child.* "Not true, you'll see. Mr. Weiss is having grilled cheese just like you!" *Well, that's decided, then.*

"Bracha, do you like the new skirt I'm wearing? Got it on sale at Loehmann's, some astounding designer price normally, but I picked it up for only twenty-three dollars — a steal!"

Devoiry twirled around to show off her long, bright purple and blue polyester skirt, eminently practical and washable to withstand constant exposure to multiple kitchen experiments. Ruining her wardrobe was one of the hazards of her profession, so she was always on the lookout for inexpensive, *tznius* clothing.

"Pretty, Mom, love the colors. Looks great on you."

"Thanks. I'm going to check on Malka. Please clean up your dishes after you're done. I'm not the maid. You know where the dairy dishwasher is."

"You wouldn't want me to get 'em mixed up and put the cheese plate in the *fleishig* dishwasher, right, Mommy?" Tully joked.

"I'll take my chances, buddy. Just do it."

Why is it that I miss my children so much all day long, but then, in the span of five minutes, I want to send them all to their rooms?

As Devoiry headed upstairs, Bracha called out to her. "Mommy, Tatty is on the phone. He says he has to talk to you right away." Bracha crossed the room to hand the cordless to Devoiry, who had paused on the stairs.

Oh, no, what happened? Devoiry grabbed the receiver. "Hi, dear. What's the matter? Everything okay?"

"Well, sort of. I have to talk to you about this bill I'm paying."

Something in his stern tone sent a chill through Devoiry's spine. *I thought we had plenty of money in the bank. Isn't Yossi's business doing great?*

"You mean the tuition bill, dear? You must be looking at the building fund they add on every January. That's why it's higher than usual," she replied, forcing herself to keep her voice calm and measured. Money conversations often got Yossi agitated, so Devoiry tried to avoid them at all costs.

"No, nothing to do with tuition. I haven't paid that one yet. Right now I'm paying the water bill. (*You've got to be kidding, this is the big emergency?*) I looked at last month's bill, and it was $92, and this month, the bill is $106. What's going on? Do we need to talk to Bracha again about not taking such long showers?"

Stay calm. Very calm.

"I can see why you're upset, dear. Fourteen dollars is a lot of money to pour down the drain." *It's a good thing the latest grocery bill was paid in cash.*

"I'll speak to Bracha, don't worry, honey," she

said, trying to console him. *Yikes, if he only knew how much money I'm spending every day trying to come up with kosher recipes that will sell.*

Yossi continued. "Talk to all the kids and remind them — they must turn the water off while they are soaping up and only turn it on to wash the soap away. That fourteen dollars we wasted could buy a day's worth of groceries!"

Grilled cheese sandwiches, maybe. When is he going to learn? He likes to brag about his wife, the kosher celebrity, but Heaven forbid he should find out about the kind of money it takes to create a star. He would plotz!

Devoiry's head was starting to pound, that aggravating, pulsating pain that starts over her right eye and renders her incapacitated in an hour if she doesn't down three Advils pronto. "I'll see you later tonight, dear. Remember that Mr. Weiss is coming for dinner. Don't forget to come home soon so you can be here, okay? Gotta go."

"Yeah, it's Tuesday, I know. All right, I'll leave now. We can live it up a bit for tonight's dinner. I landed a big kahuna today. *Frum* guy from Toronto, running a two million dollar operation and he's lost total control of his finances. I can save him a ton. Expense Reduction Associates to the rescue! Give me the chance, and I'll save you way more money than it'll cost you to hire me."

Amazing how happy he sounds whenever he's

talking about saving money. Now, if he'd only leave me alone about it. One minute it's "Bring out the wine and let's celebrate," and a minute later it's "Why did you buy this wine for $15.99 when they have it on sale at Rite Aid for $9.99?

"Terrific, I'm so proud of you. I'm sure you're going to do great things for him. See you soon, dear."

Devoiry walked the phone back downstairs to the receiver, grabbed the bottle of Advil sitting on the counter next to the spices and the vitamins, and downed three tablets before heading back upstairs to deal with Malka's new crisis of the day.

"You fighting with Tatty about money again, Mom? Whenever you go for the Advil, it's usually after you and Tatty had an argument," Bracha pointed out as she took a seat at the kitchen bar, looking for her dinner.

"No, dear, no argument. You know how Tatty can be sometimes. But it's because he works so hard to take care of us, and he hates to see any of our money wasted. Just be a little more careful about keeping showers short while he's focused on the water bill, okay?"

"Yeah, whatever. Hope your headache goes away, Mom. I hate having headaches," Bracha responded. "And I hate it when you get a headache — you're no fun at all."

"Me, too. I'll be okay. You know how to use

the sandwich maker. Can you make yourself some dinner? I have to get Malka calmed down and then put together a real meal for Tatty and Mr. Weiss, and Mordy will be home from yeshivah at 9, and you know how he's always *starving* when he walks in the door."

Devoiry headed back to the staircase, wishing the Advil would kick in within seconds instead of minutes. *What I really want to do right now is go to bed!*

"No problem. I'll feed myself," Bracha muttered.

Bracha was never one to keep her feelings to herself, as Devoiry was reminded when she heard Bracha kvetching to Tully: "Mom made *you* a sandwich, and you know she'll cook up something amazing for Mr. Weiss, and of *course,* Malka gets all the attention. What about me?"

Devoiry glanced over her shoulder to see Tully leaping off of his barstool to hug Bracha with one of his can't-be-resisted, full-of-enthusiasm bear hugs.

"Sis, you get *me*! Wanna make me another sandwich while you're making yours? Play a game of checkers with me? Help me with my homework?"

Devoiry chuckled. *Tully, my ice breaker. Even Bracha won't be able to stay mad for long with you around! Now what are we going to do with poor Malka?*

She listened carefully as she plodded up the stairs, dreading another dramatic scene with Malka. *Good, no sobbing sounds. Maybe she's calmed herself down.* Sometimes, *not* rushing to her side was the best solution.

Two

Stopping in the doorway of Malka and Bracha's room, Devoiry noticed Malka's face buried in her pillow, but the sobbing had stopped. Now there was just the erratic breathing that follows a preteen's temper tantrum.

"Malka, sugar," Devoiry knelt down to cuddle her on the bottom bunk, careful not to bang her already-pounding head on the bunk's frame. "What happened today that got you so upset?"

Malka peeked out from below her pillow, her eyelids swollen from a ten-minute-solid crying jag. "It's no use, Ma. Don't waste your money on me anymore. Just homeschool me and I'll help you in the kitchen and grow up to be a famous chef like you."

Devoiry tried to placate her. "But you're so smart. What about all that learning you'd miss?"

"I don't need to learn stupid science or math or English! I can just cook for people like you do and make them happy and not have to worry about grades, or tests, or my dumb twitches!"

"Aw, honey, sounds like you had a really rough day. Tell me about it."

Malka rolled over, and Devoiry noticed that Malka's eyelids were blinking very rapidly and her neck jerked to the right with regular spasms she couldn't control. She resisted the urge to tell Malka to stop, as if Malka's spasms were under her control.

"Bad day with the twitches, huh? Tell me about it."

"It was the worst! I was so freaked out in science, because the mean teacher makes me so nervous I forget everything I learned, and when I started taking the test, my neck kept jerking around, and then Sashi, the smartest girl in the class, who sits behind me, she went up to the teacher and told her that I was cheating because I kept looking at her paper, except I wasn't cheating at all, I was just twitching, and it looked like I was cheating, 'cause my head kept jerking back as if I was looking at her paper but I wasn't, I *promise* I wasn't, and I told the teacher that, but I don't know if she believed me, and I didn't want to say to her that it was my twitches, it was *so* embarrassing, and then my eyes kept blinking and I couldn't see the paper because everything was blurry and the time went so fast, and I didn't even get to answer half the questions and I just know that I failed this test, Ma, but I studied so so so hard, and it's not fair, and I'm so stupid I can't stand myself, and why can't I be more like Bracha who gets A plus plus plus on everything, it's not fair!" Malka exhaled deeply.

"I can't imagine how frustrating that must have been for you. It's hard enough for you to take tests, because you get so scared, but then to be accused of cheating in the middle of the test? Ouch, that had to hurt!"

Malka sniffled and shrugged. "It was pretty bad. I hate school!"

Before Devoiry could even respond, she was surprised to hear Malka ask, "Ma, what's for dinner? I'm starving!"

Operation Rescue returns to standby. "Ah, grilled cheese. How's that sound?"

Malka popped out of bed. "Yum. You haven't made grilled cheese in ages, so can I have one now?"

Devoiry straightened, thankful that the Advil had started to work its magic. "Hug?" Devoiry reached out and drew Malka to her chest, marveling at how much taller she seemed to get every day. "Malka darling, if you keep growing, you're going to be taller than Mordy!"

Malka groaned. "Great. I'll be the twitching giraffe! They can charge admission for me at the zoo!"

Malka reached out and gave Devoiry another quick hug.

Devoiry followed Malka out of the room. "Let's go downstairs and turn out some sandwiches. I have Mr. Weiss coming in a half hour. Think you can help me turn boring, basic grilled cheese into gourmet dairy phenomenal?" asked Devoiry.

Malka's face lit up. "Sure, Mom. I'll be your helper. You watch, it'll be great!"

Amazing. I let her vent for sixty seconds, and her exuberance returns. My beautiful Malka, I wish I could help you smile at school and not just at home. It's a good thing we have that meeting with the principal Monday morning. Hope it will help.

As Devoiry entered the kitchen, she was relieved to see that Bracha was busy with homework on the dining room table and Tully was practicing his guitar, a new passion of his since he received it for Chanukah.

"Listen, Mommy, listen, listen, *listen*. Don't I sound like Yaakov Shwekey?" Tully vigorously ran his guitar pick up and down the strings, producing an eight-year-old boy's version of a *niggun*.

Perfect for the headache. Thanks, Tully.

"Awesome. Tully. Keep playing for me while I make dinner for Tatty and Mr. Weiss, just a bit quieter, okay? Mommy's got a headache. I can't believe how far you've come on your own in just a couple of weeks. You know, Mr. Weiss used to play the guitar. Maybe he could give you lessons."

"*Mom,* he's *so* old. What is he, like ninety? He won't teach me anything cool. I want to be an awesome, rock-and-rolling kosher dude, like Lipa Schmeltzer."

Devoiry chuckled. "Okay, dude, let's see what we can figure out. Maybe Mr. Weiss can recommend someone for you. He's only in his sixties. Not exactly ancient, but yeah, Lipa Schmeltzer probably isn't on his iPod!"

"*Mom,* guys as old as him don't even *have* iPods. They listen to the radio!"

Devoiry strode to where Tully was parked on the couch, guitar in hand. "Tully, I have a *big* favor to ask of you." She sat herself on the rim of the couch next to him.

"Mom, can't you see I'm busy making my first album?" Tully grinned.

"Yes, exactly. I know that you don't really need Mr. Weiss to be your teacher — but you see, Mr. Weiss really needs you. He's so lonely since Mrs. Weiss passed away. He spends a lot of his time by himself. It would be such big fun for him to play guitar with you, and you don't have to tell him that you really don't need his help. You can *pretend* that you need him to teach you. Then, when we help

Mr. Weiss find a new wife and he's not lonely anymore, we can get you a cool dude teacher. What d'ya say? I think you'll be surprised at how much you could learn from him."

Tully shrugged. "Okay, I like Mr. Weiss. He's always nice to me and he's funny, too. I'll do it. I'll let him be my teacher and I'll pretend to like it. But as soon as you find him a wife, I get my own, for-real guitar teacher, okay?"

Devoiry stuck out her hand to shake Naftali's, and he pumped it hard. Noticing 6:55 on the wall clock, she jumped off the couch.

"Malka, Mr. Weiss will be here in five minutes. Let's get cracking here. Plug in the sandwich maker and run downstairs to the freezer and grab the Italian bread. Let me show you how to make a grilled cheese that'll make Mr. Weiss and Tatty ask for seconds!"

"Dokee okee!" Malka replied. She reappeared a moment later with bread in hand.

"Malka, let me show you the secret." Devoiry took out a skillet big enough for four pieces of bread facedown. "It's in the butter and garlic. Melt some butter in the frying pan, drop in a tablespoon of crushed garlic, and coat the bread in it before it goes into the maker. Use only the best mozzarella, sprinkle some basil and oregano inside the sandwich before it goes in — voilà, grilled cheese transformed into respectable dinner."

"Mommy, can I *please* cut the cheese with the cheese slicer? That's so much fun!"

Devoiry startled when the doorbell rang. "Sure, dear, use the dairy cutting board and the slicer, and grab the cheese out of the bin."

"Bracha, doorbell. Must be Mr. Weiss. Can you let him in, please?"

"Sure. No problem." Bracha walked to the foyer to open the door and was practically knocked over as the door swung open just as she was reaching for it.

"Tatty! Mr. Weiss!"

"Hey, honey. I just happened to come home as Mr. Weiss got here. Bracha, please take Mr. Weiss's coat and hang it up for him."

"Thank you, Bracha." Mr. Weiss said as he removed his long black coat and handed it to her. "Is this too heavy for you?"

"No, I'm fine."

Mrs. Rosenberg, it smells like Gan Eden in here. Can't wait!"

"Thanks, Mr. Weiss. Nothing special, just a grilled cheese. Please forgive me. The day got away from me. Dinner will be ready in a few." Devoiry headed for the kitchen to finish off the dinner.

"Mr. Weiss, come quick," called Naftali from the living room, still sitting on the couch with his guitar. "You gotta hear me play. Mommy says I'm really good. She says you used to play guitar."

"Let me see what you've got here, Tully." Mr. Weiss plopped his sizable frame on the couch next to Naftali. Naftali thrust his guitar into Mr. Weiss's hands.

"Here, play! Mommy told me you know how."

"Well, it's been a very long time, but your mommy is right, I used to play. Let me see if my fingers still remember what to do."

As Mr. Weiss's hands began strumming and finger picking, Naftali sat up and took notice. "Wow, you're really good! Will you teach me how to do that?"

"Well, you probably want to find yourself a real teacher," Mr. Weiss demurred.

Naftali hugged Mr. Weiss and exclaimed, "You *are* a real teacher! Here, teach me right now. Show me how to play that song."

"Tully, let's get Mr. Weiss some dinner first, then maybe after dinner, okay? We want him to be able to eat his grilled cheese while it's hot. Mr. Weiss, please sit in your usual spot. Your sandwich is ready."

"Thank you so much. You have no idea how much I look forward to these Tuesday nights. Other than Shabbos, it's the best meal of the week for sure!" Mr. Weiss smiled.

"If it weren't for you, I'd be living on the chicken and rice from the Glatt Mart in town." Mr. Weiss stretched his long frame and got off the couch.

"Oh, it's really our pleasure. Yossi, grilled cheese for you, too?"

"Fabulous. Smells great!"

Yossi and Mr. Weiss settled down at the kitchen table. Devoiry placed two grilled-to-perfection golden cheese sandwiches on her nice plates, garnished them with a sprig of salad greens, and asked Bracha to serve the men.

"Here you go, Mr. Weiss, and here you go, Tatty," Bracha said as she placed their plates in front of them. The men went to the kitchen sink to wash and say their *berachos*. They returned to the table and took their first bites.

"Wow. Phenomenal!" Mr. Weiss raved. "You're the only person I know that can turn a simple grilled cheese into gourmet cuisine. Oh, how I miss Tzipporah's cooking! She had such a knack in the kitchen. Nothing like her Shabbos cholent!"

"I remember her cholent — yes, it was always *geshmack*," Yossi commented.

Mr. Weiss's eyes glazed over. "I can still taste it, even though it's been over a year. She always amazed me, the way she'd toss a bunch of simple ingredients into a pot and turn out such a meal. Boy, I really miss her."

"Ima, are you going to eat something?" Yossi asked. *Good diversion, Yossi. Don't want Mr. Weiss to get all mopey.*

"Later, dear. I'll eat with Mordy. I was sampling

all afternoon, so I'm not really hungry."

"Ah, what were you cooking up? Anything for us to try?"

Oops, shouldn't have said anything. "Not quite ready yet, dear. But when it is, you'll be the first to know."

Devoiry walked over to where the men were sitting. "So, Mr. Weiss," Devoiry said, "how'd your date go with Mrs. Saperstein? I understand the two of you met for coffee on Sunday."

Mr. Weiss leaned back in his chair and furrowed his gray, bushy eyebrows. "Well...she's a very pleasant person."

The silence stretched long enough; Devoiry understood. Mr. Weiss would never speak ill of anyone. This *shidduch* was going nowhere.

"Okay. Got it. Yossi, did you ever find out if the lawyer who works in your building knows anyone for Mr. Weiss to meet? He's so well connected."

After eating the sandwich with gusto, Yossi patted his ample belly in satisfaction. "No, I'll have to track him down. Jacob, we have to find you a missus who can put together a meal as fine as my wife does. Ima, can I have another sandwich, please? Jacob, another?"

"Sure," Devoiry replied. *My own husband loves a simple grilled cheese. Why do I keep trying to do kosher gourmet?*

"No more for me," said Mr. Weiss. "I'm full.

Mind if I *bentch* and then see if I can teach Tully a thing or two on the guitar?"

"That would be terrific. Thanks," Devoiry said as she prepared Yossi a second sandwich.

When the sandwich was ready and Mr. Weiss was out of earshot, she sat down next to him at the kitchen table, placed his sandwich in front of him, and spoke softly. "What do you think he meant by 'She's a very pleasant person.'"

"He didn't like her, but he doesn't want to tell you that."

"Well, he said she was pleasant. What's wrong with pleasant? Maybe he's just being too picky. There was that widow — classy, smart woman. Okay, a little pudgy, but she's a lovely person. And remember Harold's sister? Okay, she chatters a lot, but he's lonely! Seems like whoever we introduce him to, she's never able to hold a candle to Tzipporah."

Yossi wiped the crumbs off his chin from the second sandwich, which he consumed as fast as the first one.

"'Pleasant' is another word for 'boring.' Jacob's brilliant. He needs a real conversationalist, and someone who can handle the fact that he's six foot six! Not to mention that Tzipporah was almost as good as you are in the kitchen. Not so easy to find him a new wife...but Hashem is great, and He'll figure it out. We'll just keep our eyes out for him.

Hashem will part this Red Sea, don't worry."

"Mom," Malka called out from the homework table where she was studiously preparing for a math test the next day. "Phone call. It's Mrs. Weiner from down the block."

Probably fund-raising for one thing or another. G-d bless her, she has her finger in just about every pie in this community.

"Okay. I'll pick it up in the kitchen."

Devoiry greeted her while immersing her hands in soapy water. "Mrs. Weiner, how are you?"

"*Baruch Hashem,* can't complain. Or I could, but what good would it do?" she cackled. "Listen, I have a very delicate situation to talk to you about. Is this a good time?"

Devoiry stopped the running water so she could hear Mrs. Weiner, who was getting on in age and not always easily understood. "Delicate, did you say? What's up?" she asked while drying her hands on a dish towel.

Mrs. Weiner hesitated, then began. "Well, you see, it's about your Mordy."

"What about him?" *What could she possibly know about my Mordy?*

"Well, if I had knowledge that Mordy is having some trouble at school, would you want to know?"

Devoiry felt her face flush, and she sat down on the kitchen barstool. "What are you talking about,

Mrs. Weiner? Mordy is doing great at yeshivah!"

"Remember that bad storm we had a while ago? Brought us lots of ice and power outages?"

"Sure, it was an ice-skating rink out there. What's this got to do with my Mordy?" Devoiry asked impatiently.

"Well, it appears that you and I have a phone problem now."

Devoiry's jaw clenched. "Phone problem?"

Mrs. Weiner cleared her throat. "Well, seems our lines are crossed. I called you the other day to see if you wanted to make a meal for Mrs. Harrison. You know, she just had her gall bladder out, and then she developed an infection, and she's had a tough time with all those kids, so anyway, I'm organizing meals for her, and I called you because of course, you're an amazing cook and I know she'd love a meal from you and..." She took a deep breath and continued... "and when I called you, it was the strangest thing. Mordy was on the phone talking to his friend Shmueli, and they didn't know I was on the line, and I kept saying, 'Hello, hello' but they couldn't hear me, even though I could hear every word they were saying. Just like the old days — a party line! You know, I'm almost old enough I remember those days." Mrs. Weiner laughed.

"You were listening to Mordy's conversation on the phone?" Devoiry's responded in a shrill voice. *Dear G-d, what did she hear, and who did she tell?*

"Well, Devoiry, it's not like I wanted to listen. I mean, it was never my intention to eavesdrop. But I just couldn't help it. Mordy was talking to his friend, and they didn't realize I was on the phone. So anyway, do you want me to tell you what I heard?"

Laws of lashon hara. What are they? Come on, I've learned these laws for years. Benefit of the doubt. Don't listen to anything that could be rechilus.

"It seems that you've called me to tell me something important, but I'm not comfortable with this conversation," Devoiry said, as she stabbed a fork over and over again into a paper napkin, tearing it to shreds. "I would feel best if I talked to Mordy directly."

"I think you should know," Mrs. Weiner plowed on further, "that Mordy is —"

"Mrs. Weiner," Devoiry interrupted. "Please, I don't want to discuss this. I'm sure you don't want to gossip, and I don't want to listen to it."

Devoiry rose and started pacing the length of the kitchen island and back. "Mrs. Weiner, first of all, I must tell you, this is all quite upsetting to me. We must get the phone problem fixed immediately. I am sure you want your phone privacy as much as we do. I thank you for your concern, and I'm going to return to my dinner now. And oh, yes, I'm happy to cook a meal for Mrs. Harrison. Just tell me what you need."

"Tsk, tsk, if you had heard what I heard, you'd be very concerned. I suggest you talk with your Mordy very soon. Such a fine, fine boy. And meanwhile, of course, I will keep this in the highest confidence. I know how private you are."

"Thank you. I appreciate it. I'll call the phone company in the morning. Good night, Mrs. Weiner."

The nerve of that woman, listening in on a conversation that was none of her business!

Devoiry hung up the phone, pausing before her first inclination, which was to rush into the dining room to tell Yossi all about Mrs. Weiner's unwelcome call.

I have to hear it straight from Mordy before I speak to Yossi about it. Mordy should be home soon. What's going on?

Devoiry wrote in big letters on a dry-erase message board on her fridge: First Thing, Call Phone Repair!"

Three

"SMELLS GREAT IN HERE. WHAT'S for dinner? I'm starved," Mordy called out as he strode into the house. He threw his backpack in its usual place on the foyer floor and tossed his winter jacket on the couch on the way to the kitchen.

"Mordy, how many times do I have to tell you? Hang up your coat in the hall closet, and don't throw your backpack where people will trip over it!" Devoiry greeted him.

"In a minute," he responded, peering into the kitchen to see what was on the menu.

"Do it now!" Devoiry said, rubbing her temples.

"Whoa. Okay, okay. I'll do it now. Bad day in the kitchen, Ima?"

"Just because I ask you not to be a slob in this house doesn't mean I'm having a bad day," she said. *Oh, gosh! Forgot Mr. Weiss is here.*

Mordy put his hands up in mock surrender. "Right, okay. Whatever... Hi, Tatty. Hi, Mr. Weiss. How is everybody?"

Mr. Weiss reached out his hand to shake Mordy's as he walked back through the living room to hang up his coat. "Just fine. Your Ima cooked up another fabulous meal. Boy, you're lucky to be eating her meals every day!"

Mr. Weiss stood up from the couch. "Yossi, Rabbi Rosen is giving the eight o'clock *Daf Yomi*. After *ma'ariv* will you stay for the *shiur*?"

Yossi stretched and got up from the table. "Yes, I just *bentched,* and I like to get to Rabbi Rosen's *shiur* whenever I can. Any problem with that, Ima?"

Great. Gives me a chance to talk to Mordy. "No, of course not. Enjoy!" Devoiry left the kitchen to get Mr. Weiss his coat. She lifted his coat off its hanger.

"Hmmm, if I had a cashmere coat, I might even look forward to winter!" she exclaimed as she handed it to Mr. Weiss.

A woman can dream. Yossi would never go for it as long as Land's End offers a lifetime guarantee.

Mr. Weiss took the coat from Devoiry and reached his long arms through the sleeves, buttoning it up to the collar and slipping on his leather gloves. "Yossi, want to ride with me?"

"Sure. Appreciate saving on the gas. Everyone should be carpooling. Then we wouldn't have such a fuel problem."

"We look forward to seeing you again this Shabbos for lunch, right, Mr. Weiss?" asked Devoiry. "We'll have another guest as well. Jessica is a senior at Franklin and Marshall College, active with Hillel, very curious, but hesitant. We have her staying with us this Shabbos. She could learn a lot from you."

"I'm grateful for the invitation. I'd never turn down a meal in your home, especially on Shabbos. I'll walk over with Yossi after shul. Thanks so much."

Yossi donned his black hat and his fifteen-year-old winter coat that still worked fine except for occasional zipper problems, and wrapped the scarf Devoiry knitted for him around his neck.

"Thanks again for this scarf. Really appreciate it. You saved us a lot of money by making it yourself, and it's keeping me warm."

"My pleasure." *That was an act of caring, not of cost cutting.*

"Let's go, Jacob," Yossi said as he opened the front door. "We don't want to be late for *V'hu Rachum*. See you at about 9:20, Ima. Say good night to the girls for me if they're in bed before I'm home," he said.

"Bye, Mordy," Yossi called. "G'night, Tully. Great guitar playing tonight!"

"Thanks, Tatty." Naftali lifted his guitar up into the air. "Mr. Weiss is teaching me a new song!"

The men left and Devoiry closed the front door behind them to keep out the winter chill. "Mordy, come into the kitchen and I'll put together a sandwich for you."

"A sandwich for dinner? You must have had a really bad day!" he joked.

Devoiry bristled. "Mordy, my day was perfectly fine, and what's wrong with a sandwich? The rest of the family had no complaints!" Devoiry inhaled deeply and then exhaled.

Calm down. You don't even know if he did anything wrong.

"Sorry, Mordy. I don't mean to sound off like that. Actually, there's something on my mind. Let me make you that sandwich and then we'll talk."

Mordy stared at Devoiry, a worried look crossing his face. "What's the matter, Ima? I don't want to eat till you tell me what's up. Now you have me worried."

"Okay, let's talk first. Then once we get something cleared up, I'll make you the most delicious grilled cheese you've ever eaten!"

Mordy grinned. "Fantastic. Make me three of them. I'm really hungry!"

"Bracha! Malka!" Devoiry called. "Mordy and I

are going into Tatty's study to talk. Leave us be for a while, okay?"

"Uh-oh, Mordy's in big trouble!" Bracha shouted gleefully. "Okay, Mommy, we won't bother you. Good luck, Mordy!"

"Ima, you never go into Tatty's study. What did I do?" Mordy followed Devoiry into Yossi's private study, down the hallway, and away from the curious ears of his sisters.

As they entered the study, Devoiry closed the heavy, dark-stained wood door behind them. *There's something about all these sefarim lining the shelves. I feel calmer already.*

Mordy took a seat on the small couch in front of Yossi's sizable mahogany desk.

"Ima, some day I want a study just like this, with *sefarim* covering every square inch of wall space, and people calling me day and night to ask me *shailahs*, and I'll know just which *sefer* to look in for the answer!"

"Amen!"

Mordy leaned toward Devoiry, who had taken a seat on Tatty's favorite overstuffed leather chair, the place he often fell asleep with a *sefer* on his lap. She rarely sat in his chair, but she knew he wouldn't mind, and she found strength in it.

"Mordy, how's everything going in yeshivah?"

"Great. I love it there." He wriggled in his seat. "Why?"

"That's what I thought, too," Devoiry nervously tapped her forefinger against her top lip and continued. "I was puzzled by a conversation I had earlier this evening with our neighbor. I just want to be sure you're not in any kind of trouble."

Mordy's eyebrows arched. "What does our neighbor have to say about me and yeshivah? I go to school an hour away. Who would have a clue?"

"Yes, it is strange. Seems we have a phone problem since the last ice storm, and unbeknownst to us, one of our neighbors can listen in on our phone conversations."

"What do you mean?"

"When she calls our house, if we're on the phone, she can listen in on the conversation, and we don't even know she's there."

Mordy leaned back on the couch and whistled. "So, what did she hear? You're upset about something. What did I say?"

"Probably nothing. I'll tell you which conversation she overheard, without any details, and you tell me what it was about, okay?"

"Oh, I know. She probably heard me saying some *lashon hara* when I talk to my friends. Sorry, Ima, I'm working on that. I know I could do better with my *shemiras halashon*, being a *yeshivah bachur* and all. It's just something we guys do sometimes when we're talking to each other — never in front of the rebbe'im, of course. But anyway, what business is this of hers?"

"Actually, none of this is her business. I agree. But, that's not what this is about. Thanks for coming clean about the language though." Devoiry smiled.

"Stop holding out on me, Ima. What's got you so worried?"

"Well, I didn't want to listen to *lashon hara* or *rechilus*, so I wouldn't let her tell me anything. All she got out was that she heard something in your conversation with Shmueli and she thought I would be concerned if I knew. Any idea what she's talking about?"

Mordy was silent for a moment, and Devoiry let him revisit the conversation. Then she saw awareness crossing his face.

"I think I know, Ima, but she completely misunderstood. The other night me and Shmueli were talking on the phone. She was listening? Oh, that's *so* creepy. Anyway, there's nothing for you to worry about. I'm not cheating at all. Don't you trust me?"

Devoiry's voice rose an octave. "Cheating? Why would she think you're cheating?"

"I was talking to Shmueli about him helping me write my Holocaust research paper. She must think that I was having Shmueli write it for me, but it's not like that at all!"

Devoiry fell back into the soft chair and allowed the feeling of relief to flood her body. "Why don't you tell me what you have going on with Shmueli?"

Mordy stood and started pacing the small study from one end or another, nervously biting his lip.

"Ima, you know that English is a problem for me, right? My yeshivah didn't exactly do the best job preparing me for high school English. So, Shmueli is having trouble in Gemara and I love Gemara, and Shmueli is a fantastic writer, so he and I are swapping."

"Swapping what?"

"Well, every week, I help Shmueli with his Gemara, and then when I have a paper to write for my English studies, Shmueli looks it over and gives me corrections — kind of like having my own personal spell-checker! But it's totally legit, Ima. He's not writing the papers for me. He's just saving me the embarrassment of turning in a paper that a fourth grader would write!"

Mordy grabbed a paperweight off Yossi's desk, and started throwing the paperweight back and forth between his hands.

Devoiry winced. "Careful, Mordy, we don't want that paperweight to break! Remember I got it in Israel?"

"Ima, what was our neighbor doing poking her nose in my business, and where does she get off accusing me of cheating?"

Devoiry nodded. "This is the danger of *rechilus*.

She didn't accuse you of cheating. She just called me to tell me that there was something I should be asking you about. She must have heard you talking to Shmueli about him fixing up your English paper and she came to the wrong conclusion. I'm sure she had positive intentions when she called me."

Mordy humphed. "Yeah, right. Positive intentions. She was stirring the pot and making trouble!"

"I understand why you're upset. I was, too. I'm calling the phone company first thing tomorrow."

Mordy put the paperweight back on the desk and turned back toward his mother. "Okay, I'll just be grateful that you and I got this straight, and I will judge her *l'kaf zechus*. No harm done, it's just spooky to think that this lady has been eavesdropping on me, making you think I'm a cheater."

Devoiry squirmed in the comfy chair, which suddenly wasn't feeling as comfortable. "Mordy, I'm not accusing you of cheating, I'm really not. But I just have to ask you this question. Is your friend Shmueli rewriting your papers for you, and then you're turning them in, or is he just giving you a bit of tutoring, you know, '*i* before *e*, not after *c*' kind of help?"

Mordy's face flushed and he immediately looked away from Devoiry toward the wall. "I told you, Ima, he's just helping me. Why don't you believe me? You trust that nosy neighbor of ours more than me?"

"I do not think that you are intentionally cheating," Devoiry said in measured tones. "But I'm going to ask you the question again and I want an honest answer. Are you asking Shmueli to rewrite your papers, and then turning them in as if it's your own work, or is Shmueli just offering you suggestions for improvement, but the papers you're handing in are honestly coming from your effort?

Mordy paced the width of the room, and Devoiry didn't push him for an immediate answer. *Please, G-d, don't let Mordy be a cheater.*

Mordy flopped back down on the couch, his face crumpling. "You can't tell Tatty, he'll be furious with me. He'll ground me for like forever. Please, Ima, don't tell Tatty!"

Tears welled up in Devoiry's eyes. *Mordy was always the good one.* "Mordy, what happened? If you were having such trouble in your English studies, why didn't you come to us and tell us you need help? We can hire you a tutor or talk to your rebbe'im; I'm sure we can help, so you don't have to rely on Shmueli."

For a second, Mordy's eyes flashed with anger.

"Because it might cost money, that's why. I don't want to deal with Tatty and how he feels about anyone wasting a nickel. He'll just give me a whole *mussar shmuess* about how I should have paid better attention in school, and he already pays so much money for yeshivah, and why should he have to pay extra for private tutoring when I should've learned this on my own."

"Oh, sweetie." Devoiry instinctively reached over to touch his cheek, which was burning red with shame. She looked him in the eye. "I know Tatty can be difficult around money, but we're both so proud of you and how well you're doing in yeshivah. If this is holding you back..."

"It's not holding me back! If Mrs. Nosybody down the block hadn't been butting in where she doesn't belong, you and Tatty wouldn't have known the difference. I don't need to write anyway to be a rebbe, and I'm acing all my Hebrew classes. Just leave it alone, Ima. Don't mess up my system!"

"Mordy," Devoiry replied quietly, "your system is a form of lying, and it can't continue. The A grades you collect in Gemara class matter a lot less to me than whether you turn out to be a mensch or not."

"You can't do this, Ima! I'm finished! I'll fail my English class, and everyone will know how stupid I am! Pleeeease, let me handle it!"

Devoiry took a deep breath. What would Yossi say? "Mordy, I know you had positive intentions. You didn't want to let me or Tatty down, and you want your rebbes to think you're really smart. You *are* really smart — smart enough to know that you've been walking a line here and have not been totally honest, and it's time to come clean.

Mordy's eyes widened and his voice trembled.

"What do you mean, come clean? You can't make me tell the rebbe'im. I'll be humiliated."

Devoiry paused to think through a plan. "How many papers have you turned in that were mostly Shmueli's work?"

Mordy leaned back and closed his eyes, counting on his fingers. Thumb, index finger... *Please G-d, make it only one hand's worth.*

"Only three, and really, one of them was totally mine, and he just helped me a little. And the second one was maybe up to the line, but not crossing it. But yeah, the third one, my history report, that one...you're right. Too many tests that week. I just let Shmueli rewrite it and then I turned it in with my name on it." Mordy shrugged. "Guess I'm not *perfect* boy, after all." He looked down at his knees.

"Mordy, your Tatty and I never expect you to be perfect. Listen, you can't imagine how many recipes I wreck before I come up with the right one."

"Yeah, but you aren't being graded on your recipes, and Tatty doesn't give you that look when you mess up, like —" his face contorted in anger — 'For this disaster, I'm paying all this money?' "

Devoiry couldn't help laughing. "You should have seen the look on his face when he tasted my bourbon chicken that was supposed to be to-die-for, so I used his most expensive bourbon, seventy-five dollars a bottle, Highland Park 12, and I only used one cup of it, but I burned the chicken and it was awful. From now on, I only use cheap bourbon for my recipes!"

Mordy gave a slight smile.

"You know what I've come to understand about your Tatty? That look you're referring to, it's just because he cares so much about being a decent, frugal Jew. He's really a good man. But this isn't about Tatty; it's about you. Mordy, what do you suggest we do to make this right?"

Mordy was silent for a moment and then he offered a solution. "I'll rewrite the history paper again as my own, and I'll come clean to my teacher, I promise, but please let *me* handle this. It'll be so humiliating if you swing into action and call a teacher conference or something."

"And what about going forward?"

"Shmueli really needs the help in Gemara, and he'd be embarrassed to take up my time if he wasn't giving me something in return. He doesn't want to be a *chesed* case. I'll keep up the swap with him, but I won't let this happen again. I'll just take his help, and then write my own paper. Okay?" Mordy asked. "Pleeease, don't tell Tatty about this. Give me a chance to clean it up first."

"What about getting you extra help, Mordy? We can afford it. I'll speak to Tatty about it."

"*No. Don't!*" Mordy insisted. "I can learn a lot from Shmueli, and it's free. I just can't get lazy about it and let him do the work."

"I'll give you the opportunity to make this right. I want to see your rewrite of that history paper, and the next few papers, too, so I can see that you're on track."

"All right." Mordy rose from the couch. "Ima, I'm really starving. Can you make me that grilled cheese?"

Devoiry rose out of the chair to give Mordy a big hug. "I'm so proud of you. Someday, I have no doubt, you'll be in a study twice the size of Tatty's, with *sefarim* from wall to wall!"

"Im yirtzeh Hashem!"

"Two grilled cheese sandwiches with sliced tomato, butter, and garlic, coming up!"

"Thanks, Ima. Get that phone fixed pronto!"

"I plan on it, believe me. All we need is a neighbor who likes to gossip, listening in on the Rosenberg family drama."

Four

"LIVE AGENT, LIVE AGENT, LIVE agent!" Devoiry yelled into the phone, trying to get past the computer recording intent on trapping her in the maze of automated customer service.

"You said you want to speak to a technical representative. Is that correct?" the computer confirmed in a monotone pseudo-voice.

"Yes!"

"Your waiting time will be four minutes. Your business is very important to us. We apologize for the delay," the computer voice continued.

Well, at least I got myself on the queue. Baruch Hashem for cordless phones and headsets, so waiting's not a total waste of time.

Devoiry rolled the chocolate-fudge zebra

cookies in confectioners' sugar while she tried not to listen to the irritating elevator music on the line. This recipe was a family favorite, and she always made sure she had the cookies on hand in the freezer.

Jessica will love these, and maybe I can send some back with her on motza'ei Shabbos to share with her Jewish roommate, too.

Devoiry's hands moved of their own accord, dousing the cookies in the soft white powder. With no one in the house to hear, she drowned out the "music" playing through her headset, singing out loud to one of her favorite Avraham Fried melodies:

"Hashem, please help my cookbook sell like hot cakes, and please take away those twitches from Malka, and You haven't forgotten about a *shidduch* for Mr. Weiss, right? And listen, it hasn't been going so well for me in the kitchen lately. Can You keep me from flopping at the sisterhood cooking demo coming up? Also, about Mordy —"

"This is technical support," a customer service representative said, interrupting her prayers.

"What is your phone number, please?"

"Uh, (717)-462-9997."

"Your name, please?"

"Mrs. Devoiry Rosenberg."

"Address, please?"

"118 Chalet Drive, Lancaster."

"Thank you. I see you've been a customer for four years. Thank you for your business. You are reporting a problem today, ma'am?"

I'm not old enough to be a ma'am!

"Yes. It was reported to me by my neighbor, Mrs. Weiner, who lives on the same street, that our lines have somehow crossed, and she can listen in on our conversations when she calls us if we're on the line talking."

"I'm sorry for the trouble, ma'am. How long has this problem been going on?"

"I don't know. I just learned about it yesterday. I would so appreciate it if a repair technician could come to fix this problem immediately. You can't imagine how awkward this situation is."

"I understand your concerns, ma'am."

Stop it with the ma'am business already. Just fix my phone.

"I'll schedule a technician to look at your situation as soon as possible. Let me check my schedule. You will need to be home for this repair, in case it's an inside problem. I see you have inside wiring insurance on your plan. Are you available during the day?"

"I will make myself available. This is first priority. Please give me your earliest appointment."

"Yes, ma'am. The first appointment I can give you would be next Thursday, from 8 to 12."

"What do you mean, next Thursday? That's more than a week away! We can't wait that long."

"I apologize for the inconvenience, ma'am. I am instructed to give priority to those customers who are completely without phone service, and the latest storms have created outages in some of our areas. This is the best I can do for you. Will you be available during that time, ma'am?"

Devoiry capitulated. "I guess I have no choice. I sure hope they can fix it."

"I hope so, too. I will schedule the technician for next Thursday then, from 8 to 12. Is there anything else I can help you with today, ma'am?"

"No!"

"May I transfer you to an automated survey so that you can tell us how I was able to offer you excellent customer service today, ma'am?"

"No." *You're better off not doing that.* "Thank you for your assistance." Devoiry hung up the phone.

Oy.

The doorbell startled Devoiry out of her annoyance, and she instinctively reached up to make sure that her hair was properly covered, coating her black snood in confectioners' sugar.

"Just a minute. Be right there," she called, but the kitchen was far from the front door, and the ringing persisted.

"Coming, coming," she said as she rushed to the front door, confectioners' sugar covering her hands, snood, and face.

The doorbell rang a third time. She peered through the peephole and saw the postman standing on her stoop examining a large envelope.

"Just a minute," she assured him as she opened the door, accepting the fact that she'd later have to return with some kitchen wipes to remove confectioners' sugar from the doorknob.

"Good morning, Mrs. Rosenberg. How are you today?" the postman said.

"Fine, thanks."

"Looks like you're having fun in the kitchen again!" he joked. "Cooking up anything good in there?"

"Yes, our favorite cookies. Would you like one, or is it against post office policy to eat food from your customers?"

Thanks, but I'm good. I need your signature on this certified mail. Sorry to bother you."

"No bother. What is it?" Devoiry squinted at the envelope return address, which said:

McNeil Nutritionals LLC
Splenda Recipe Competition Results
Fort Washington, PA 19034

Her heart raced. *I've been waiting for this letter, I'd almost lost hope.*

She grabbed the pen from the postman and hurriedly signed on the line.

"Thanks. Have a great day," she said.

"You're welcome. Hope those cookies come out as good as they smell!"

Devoiry's heart started pounding like a drum. She wiped her shaking hands on her apron and ripped open the envelope. Inside was an official-looking document on corporate stationery. Devoiry's eyes scanned the letter for the answer she was looking for:

> ...third-place winner...appreciate your exceptional cooking talent...your recipe was selected from thousands of submissions... tested and tasted by a committee of professional chefs...included in our next cookbook of Splenda recipes...

Devoiry's eyes raced through the contents, a wide grin pasted on her face.

"*Baruch Hashem*! Her arm shot up in the air in a sign of victory. Yes! I did it! I did it! I won!"

Inside the envelope was a check for $150. Included with the check and the letter was Devoiry's recipe, printed on an index card:

Red Cabbage Supreme	Third-Place Winner
Developed by Devoiry Rosenberg	
Prep time: 15 minutes	Total time: 1 hour
Serves 8	
1 small red cabbage, coarsely shredded	¼ red onion, finely diced
	¼ cup rice vinegar
Several baby carrots, finely diced	¼ cup olive oil
2 stalks celery, finely diced	1 palmful SPLENDA
1 cup slivered almonds	Dash of salt
Toast slivered almonds in a skillet on low heat, stirring frequently, being careful not to burn the almonds. Combine diced vegetables in a mixing bowl. Add remaining ingredients. Adjust proportions to taste. Allow to sit for at least 1 hour or overnight before serving, to blend flavors and soften cabbage.	

Devoiry rushed to the phone, noticing as she picked it up to dial that she was leaving traces of confectioners' sugar all over the headset. She forced herself to put down the phone to wash off the remnants of the sugar from her hands and shake out her snood.

The oven timer started beeping. "Okay, okay, coming!" She opened the door of the oven to find rows of perfect zebra cookies, looking and smelling as if they were made in a professional bakery.

Today is a good day.

She placed them on the stove top to cool, and then deftly placed the next tray into the oven while picking up the phone to dial Yossi.

"Come on, Yossi, pick up, pick up, pick up!"

"Expense Reduction Associates. This is Yossi Rosenberg. How may I help you save money today?" he bellowed into the phone.

"Yossi, Yossi, I won, I won, I won! The Splenda contest — I won third prize for my red cabbage recipe!"

"Wow! Mazel tov, that's terrific! You just got the news?"

"Yes, it came certified mail, with a congrats letter and a check for $150. Now we can take Malka out for a really nice dinner for her birthday on Sunday. Remember she wanted to go to her favorite Chinese restaurant in Baltimore but you didn't want to spend that kind of money? Now we can do it. Wouldn't that be fun?"

"Ah...I mean, you caught me off guard here. By the time we factor in the gas, and you know how pricey that restaurant is, and —"

"Oh, come on, Yossi. Please don't rain on my parade. I haven't won a contest in a long time. It would be so much fun to get out of town with the family, and Malka is having such a hard time these days. Let's make her feel really special. And it'll be mostly paid for! *I won*, Yossi. I'm so excited!"

"Okay," Yossi said. "I know how hard you work all day long in the kitchen. Sure, let's make it happen. You make the reservations, say, six o'clock on Sunday. Should we make it a surprise or tell her tonight?"

"Oh, let's tell her. She'll look forward to it all weekend long. We haven't been to Baltimore in ages, ever since gas got so expensive. This will be such a treat!"

"I'm proud of you. I remember that salad. You made it for Shabbos and everyone raved about it. Who knew you could make red cabbage taste so delicious? I'm not surprised at all that you won."

As they spoke, Devoiry grabbed the kitchen wipes and retraced her steps throughout the house, getting rid of the trail of confectioners' sugar she had left in her wake.

Confectioners' sugar. I bet if I made those pancakes again and left out the feta cheese and filled them with diced, cooked apples, cinnamon and sugar, and then coated them with confectioners' sugar...hmmm, reminds me of the crepes Bubby Basha used to make for us when we were kids. I should hunt up that old recipe somewhere...

"You there, Devoiry? Did I lose you?"

Yossi's voice brought her back to the moment. "Oh, sorry, dear. I was spacing out. What did you say?"

"I was just saying that I'm not at all surprised you won the contest, cause that salad was delicious! I had several helpings myself."

"Well, I'm glad the judges agreed with you. And now we'll be able to treat Malka to a really fun night. Oh, by the way, the phone company said they can't repair the phone till next Thursday. Can you believe it? That means Mrs. Weiner may be listening right now. Mrs. Weiner, are you there? Mrs. Weiner? Guess not. All right, I'll let you get back to work now. Can't wait to show you the letter and the check. See you around dinnertime, then?"

"Sounds good. Mazel tov again."

Feels so good when Yossi is proud of me.

Devoiry hung up the phone and did a little dance, reveling in the momentary feeling of success as a chef.

Wish some of my gourmet recipes would win a contest. This red cabbage recipe is a no-brainer. I threw it together in five minutes from leftovers in the fridge. But no one has to know that...

Five

"SO, JESSICA, HOW DID YOU connect up with this wonderful family?" Mr. Weiss asked as he reached for a second helping of Devoiry's famous potato kugel, a favorite of his that Devoiry always made sure was on the Shabbos table when he came for lunch.

Jessica played with the cloth napkin in her lap. "Well, that's kind of a long story, actually."

Mr. Weiss leaned his tall frame back in his chair and stretched his legs in front of him. "I don't know about you, but I've got time before *minchah*, so I'd love to hear it."

Jessica looked at Devoiry. "Go ahead, Jessica, tell him how you and I met. I love our story. It reminds me that HaKadosh Baruch Hu is really running the show."

"Exactly. It reminds *me* that I'm not really doing what I'm supposed to be doing," she mumbled, looking back down on her plate.

Devoiry sighted Naftali picking two meatballs off his plate with his chubby hands. "Naftali, get your hands out of your food. Where are your table manners?"

Naftali stuffed them into his mouth and grinned, sauce dripping down his chin. "Yummy!"

"Naftali, use a fork!"

"Mommy, I've heard this story a gazillion times, and I'm full. May I be'scused till we *bentch?*" begged Naftali, squirming in his seat.

Devoiry sighed. *I'll get him trained before shidduchim.* "Okay, you can play with your matchbox cars in the living room. But wash your hands first."

"Back at the table later with a *devar Torah,* young man," said Yossi, as Naftali scrambled off his chair and made a beeline for his favorite pastime.

"Devoiry, you make the best potato kugel I've ever tasted!" said Mr. Weiss.

"When it comes to Shabbos, there's really nothing like Bubby Basha's recipes. Zeidy Feivish always admired how creative she was in the kitchen. Her recipes are the ones my guests rave about."

Devoiry turned to Jessica. "So, Jessica, would you like to tell Mr. Weiss how you and I met?"

Jessica shrugged. "I guess I can." She looked up

from her plate in Mr. Weiss's direction.

"Well, I'm finishing my senior year in college, and I plan to be a speech therapist. In my sophomore year, I took this required course, and I always saw these four girls sticking together, wearing long skirts, long sleeves, and stockings, and it's broiling hot in our classroom. I kept waiting for one of them to break free and rebel — you know, wear a pair of pants or a T-shirt to school like the rest of us, but none of them ever did. I thought they were kind of peculiar, but...I was envious. Of their friendship, I mean. I like my blue jeans!"

"Ima, please pass the cholent," said Yossi. "Nice touch putting in the extra barley this week. I like it thick. Jessica, please continue. Sorry for the interruption," he said as he grabbed the ladle and scooped himself up a second helping of the steaming, fragrant beans and barley.

"No problem. Anyway, one day I saw one of the girls outside the bathroom mumbling something. I'd seen all the girls in the group do this many times, and I was always curious. This time I asked her, "Excuse me, but why do you always mumble something after you leave the bathroom?"

"*Asher Yatzar*," Naftali called out from the living room.

"That's right. She told me it was a prayer that Jewish people say as a thank-you to Hashem after using the bathroom. I guess she saw how shocked

I looked. Then she asked me if I was Jewish, and I said, 'Well, sort of. Not really.'"

"Don't be ridiculous," chided Bracha. "You're as Jewish as I am."

"Bracha," Devoiry said, "we don't call anyone ridiculous. You know that!"

Bracha shrugged. "Well, it's silly, that's all. Her mom's Jewish, so she's Jewish!" She punctuated her statement with a petulant stare.

Devoiry looked at Jessica. "I'm so sorry. Bracha gets like this sometimes, because it's all so clear to her, but I understand that it's not that way for you."

Bracha stood up from the table and threw her napkin on her chair. "Don't apologize for me, Ima. And don't talk about me like I'm not even in the room! You *always* do that. I'm just saying it's simple. What's all the fuss?"

"Bracha, please, watch your tone. It's Shabbos, and Jessica is our guest. Please, sit down!" Devoiry said in a tight, contorted voice.

"Bracha, that's enough! If you can't act like a proper lady at the Shabbos table, you may leave!" yelled Yossi.

Jessica's face turned pale. She twisted her long hair over and over again in her index finger.

"Fine. I don't need this. All I was trying to say is, Jessica is a Jew, period, just like us. So stop treating her like she's some kind of project or something!"

Bracha grabbed a *bentcher* from the box and started mumbling the prayer to herself while an awkward silence descended over the table.

"Jessica, I'm so sorry," Devoiry said. "It's not you. Moods of a teenager. Remember those times?"

Bracha glared up at her mother from her *bentcher* with eyes that said she'd better stop right now before she irritated Bracha even further.

Jessica face was now flushed, and she repeatedly stabbed at a green bean on her plate. She continued in a tight voice that reflected her discomfort. "I know all this seems simple to you. You all are really Jewish. My father isn't Jewish, and let's be honest here...I'm nothing like all of you."

"What my daughter was trying to say," said Yossi in a soothing, even tone, "is that according to Jewish law, since your mother is Jewish, and her mother was Jewish, and her mother, and her mother, as far as we know, all the way back to Sinai, then you're Jewish, too, and your *neshamah* is as Jewish as ours!"

Jessica half smiled and played with the earring in her right ear that hung down almost to her jawline. "That's very kind."

"Don't thank me. Thank HaKadosh Baruch Hu. He's the One who gave you your *neshamah*!" said Yossi.

"Isn't that just what I said?" Bracha said as she stomped upstairs to her room.

"So, what led you to the Rosenbergs then, Jessica?" Mr. Weiss asked, getting the conversation back on track.

"So I told this girl, her name was Shoshana, that I thought it was really beautiful that Judaism had a prayer for thanking G-d for something like using the bathroom, and she asked me if I would like to learn more, and I said, 'Okay, as long you know that I'm never going to be like you.'"

"Never say never!" piped up Malka. "That's what my Mommy always says."

Devoiry laughed. "How true. Remember how I said I would *never* publish a cookbook? And now I'm on my third one."

Jessica smiled and shook her head. "All those rules, and eating kosher, and no more pants, and being so different from everyone in my family and most of the students in my school. I'm not ready for that, but I told Shoshana that I wanted to learn more about my religion."

"So she became like a 'Partner in Torah'?" asked Mr. Weiss.

Jessica took a bite of kugel and paused. "Yes. Shoshana and I set up a time to learn every week after class, and it was amazing. I mean, I really didn't know what Judaism or the Torah was, but by learning with her, I got really interested, and then —"

"Israel!" Naftali called out again from the living room, where he was busy putting together a small city for his substantial collection of matchbox cars.

Naftali zoomed into the room with a matchbox car in hand. "Beep beep! Beep beep! Coming through! Coming through! Clear all traffic!" he yelled, swooping by the table and lifting a meatball off his plate and cramming it into his mouth before anyone could stop him. "Great meatballs, Ima!" he shouted before he zoomed back into the living room, sauce dripping down his hand and onto his once-clean white shirt.

Devoiry shook her head and threw her hands up in the air. "I officially give up my job of *derech eretz* cop," she said to Yossi. "It's your turn."

"Don't worry, he's just a kid. We'll make him respectable before he's eighteen, promise," Yossi joked.

"Like me?" asked Mordy. He leaned way across the table, stabbed a meatball with his fork from the serving bowl and said, "Don't want you to think your job is done!"

Yossi and Mr. Weiss chuckled, but Devoiry blushed. *What must Jessica and Mr. Weiss be thinking? My family is out of control today!*

"Jessica, please rescue me. Tell Mr. Weiss how you and I met. I can still remember, just a year ago, the thrill of landing on Israeli soil and everyone on the plane singing '*HaTikvah*'!"

"Continue, continue," Mr. Weiss urged her.

Jessica squirmed in her seat, looking more uncomfortable than delighted to be continuing the story.

What's wrong with her today? She seems really tense. Is it something we've done?

"Mr. Weiss, have you ever heard of Birthright?" Jessica asked.

Mr. Weiss smiled. "Sure have. That's the organization that sends Jewish kids, especially college kids, to Israel for free."

"Very worthwhile cause. I've supported them over the years, and I'm very impressed with what they've accomplished. So you were one of the lucky recipients of their free trip to Israel?"

"Yes. Shoshana convinced me to go during my summer break. To, you know, make it more real, instead of just head stuff."

"And that's where you met me and Mommy!" Bracha exclaimed, walking back into the dining room, eyes bright again, looking apologetic. "Sorry, everyone, I didn't mean to blow up." She took her seat and Devoiry decided not to respond.

Bracha continued. "Mommy took me to Israel for a vacation, just her and me, to celebrate my being bas mitzvah."

"Incredible kindness from Hashem — the trip was mostly free, too," said Yossi. "My wife won one of those raffles in a Chinese auction — an all-expenses-paid trip for two to Israel, and it was during the year of Bracha's twelfth birthday, so we decided to shelve the whole big party idea and just send Devoiry and Bracha to Israel instead."

"It was awesome," said Bracha. "I want to make aliyah when I get married. I can't wait. *Im yirtzeh Hashem,* when I'm nineteen, I'm going to marry a learner and we're going to live in Yerushalayim and I'm going to pray at the Kosel every day."

From your mouth to G-d's ears.

"Devoiry, can you pass some more of that salad please? I've never tasted such good red cabbage!" said Mr. Weiss.

"That's the recipe I won third prize for in the Splenda contest."

"Well, I can see why," he responded as he dug in for another helping.

"So, Jessica, how did you meet Mrs. Rosenberg in Israel?"

Jessica put down her fork and looked at Devoiry and Bracha. "Mrs. Rosenberg saved my life," she said quietly.

"HaKadosh Baruch Hu saved your life. I was just there as a messenger," replied Devoiry.

Jessica looked at Mr. Weiss. "Well, of course it was Hashem, but I'll always be grateful to Mrs. Rosenberg, too."

Jessica exhaled and slowly started speaking. "It was brutally hot, like 102 degrees in the shade. I hadn't eaten breakfast, I'd overslept, and my ride was leaving, so I had just enough time to get dressed, and then my friend and I went to pray at the Kosel. I felt dizzy, so I rested my head on the cool rocks. I still remember how refreshing that felt. That's the last thing I can recall.

Next thing I know, there's a crowd of people around me, and someone is putting a cold, wet napkin on my head. It's still a bit of a blur, but I remember Mrs. Rosenberg's face. She was stroking my head with this cold napkin soaked in water and saying, 'It's okay, darling, it's okay.'"

Devoiry interjected. "Bracha and I were standing right next to her. She's lucky she didn't get a concussion. I'm trained in first aid — comes in handy being the mother of four — and I figured out right away that she was breathing okay, and that she had just fainted. I took some smelling salts out of my purse —"

"You carry smelling salts? I don't know anyone who does such a thing," said Mr. Weiss.

"After a lifetime of hypoglycemia and several fainting episodes, I'm never without it," Devoiry said.

"Isn't HaKadosh Baruch Hu amazing?" said Yossi. "He places Jessica at the Kosel, and she faints right next to the only woman in the world who carries smelling salts around in her purse, who just happened to be there because she won a free trip in a Chinese auction!"

Jessica twisted her napkin so tightly that her knuckles were turning white. "When I woke up," Jessica continued, "for a few seconds, I didn't even know where I was. Mrs. Rosenberg gave me some orange juice that she had with her, and when I felt strong enough to get up and walk on my own, we started talking, and can you believe this? I find out that she lives five minutes from my college."

Jessica shook her head. "Now, if that isn't a miracle, what is?" She started mashing her kugel into something unrecognizable, looking dejected instead of elated at the realization of this blessing.

"The Creator is truly magnificent. Clearly He wanted you and the Rosenbergs to meet," declared Mr. Weiss.

Jessica took a scant swallow of water, barely wetting her lips. "I don't come as often as I should."

"The door here is always open. You know that, Jessica," Devoiry assured her. "I, too, feel that Hashem has a plan for you —"

"Yes, I know about this plan," Jessica interrupted her. "Because of the wacky way we met, and how it can't *possibly* be just a coincidence, I owe it to G-d to be like all of you — to keep all the laws, do all the mitzvos. I mean, that has to be why He hooked me up with Shoshana, and then Birthright, and now you, right? Come on, who are we kidding? You all believe that! But I...I don't know. It's such a big change, and I'm not sure I can handle it, and for sure my family can't stand the idea."

Jessica robotically moved the noodle kugel around on her plate. She looked up again, her hazel eyes focused on Devoiry. "Mrs. Rosenberg, I don't come here very often because I always feel guilty when I do. When I see all of you...I feel like a big ingrate."

Devoiry flinched. "Oh, Jessica, you've come such a long way. Remember, you used to ignore Shabbos altogether, and now you're staying with us this Shabbos so you don't have to drive. Before long —"

Jessica pushed her chair back, her face suddenly as red as the cabbage on the table. "I'm sorry," she stammered, her hands shaking. "Just because I stayed with you this Shabbos, it doesn't mean that I'm ready to keep Shabbos, and what do you mean, before long? What's the next step? You expect me to keep every Shabbos, just like you do? You don't have a clue about how hard — no, how *impossible* — this is for me! You just make it all look so easy!"

Devoiry's stomach churned with undigested cholent. "Oh, Jessica, I didn't mean to imply —

Jessica threw her napkin on the table and stood up. She looked at Devoiry, and then Yossi, her eyes brimming with tears. "Mrs. Rosenberg, Mr. Rosenberg, you've been so kind to me. Please forgive me. I'm a terrible guest. But I have to go. I'm sorry, I can't do this right now."

Devoiry quickly stood and rushed over. She reached out to touch Jessica's arm, but Jessica pulled away. "Jessica, please, please don't leave. We can help you. It's still Shabbos, don't drive, it's —"

"Yes, I know. It's *forbidden,*" Jessica retorted as she grabbed her purse, removed her keys, and opened the front door. "I can't be you. I'll never be you. I'm sorry," she cried, running down the driveway.

"Yossi, do something!" Devoiry yelled out to her husband. "We can't let her leave like this! It's still Shabbos!"

Yossi sat at the dining room table, his brown eyes calm. "Ima, there's nothing we can do right now. Let her be. The harder we push her, the farther she'll run. Hashem has a plan. You'll see."

Devoiry watched Jessica drive away. Her chest felt so tight, she could scarcely breathe. *Is this really about us, or is something else going on?*

Six

DEVOIRY HEARD A FORCEFUL KNOCK at the door, and her heart skipped a beat. "*Baruch Hashem,* Jessica came back!" she yelled out to the family sitting at the table awaiting dessert. She put down the pie that she was in the middle of slicing, calling out to Naftali, "Tully, answer the door. You're the closest."

"I thought she left!" Tully went running to the door and flung it open. "Hi, Jessica!" he shouted. Naftali wrinkled his nose and squinted. "Uh, Mrs. Weiner, you're not Jessica!"

Devoiry reached the front door, and put on her so-nice-to-see-you smile. "Mrs. Weiner, good Shabbos. What a surprise! Would you like to come in for dessert?"

"That would be lovely, dear." She placed her cane in back of her and stepped carefully into the foyer, tottering in her two-inch heels. "I hope I'm not intruding. I was so concerned when I saw that woman drive off, I just had to see if everything is all right."

"May I take your coat, Mrs. Weiner?" Devoiry asked.

"Yes, dear, be careful. It's very heavy. Real mink. My mother's, *zichronah livrachah*. Tsk, tsk, she died way too young, but I inherited her beautiful coat, the one my father, *alav hashalom*, bought her for their tenth wedding anniversary."

She handed over the coat to Devoiry, revealing an elegant suede suit with a silk kerchief tied around her neck. "You look lovely, Mrs. Weiner," said Devoiry as she hung the coat in their foyer closet. *I'm so not in a Mrs. Weiner mood.*

"Thank you, dear. These Shabbos afternoons, they can be so lonely for me, ever since I lost my Harold. So, *nu*, what happened with the girl? Why did she drive off in such a huff? I couldn't help seeing through my picture window!"

"Come, let's go in the dining room. Nothing to worry about, Mrs. Weiner. If you don't mind, I'd like to keep that situation private."

"Is there anything I can do, dear?" she said. "*Oy*, I have plenty of time on my hands these days."

"No, we're fine," she replied as they walked

slowly to the dining room, Mrs. Weiner's arm resting in the crook of Devoiry's elbow. "The girls left for B'nos — Bracha is a counselor now — and you saw Tully, but he's had enough of Shabbos table manners, so he's playing in the living room."

"Yossi, Mr. Weiss, Mordy, look who is visiting us for dessert!" she announced with forced cheer as she brought Mrs. Weiner to an empty seat at the dining room table. *Jessica's seat. I hope she's okay. I feel terrible.*

Yossi stood. "Mrs. Weiner, how did we get so lucky to have such a *chashuveh* guest? So glad you could join us!" he said, remaining standing just until she was seated with her cane resting on the arm of the chair.

"You're very kind. I'm just a lonely widow up the street, but we can pretend, can't we?" she joked. "Mordy, how is high school going for you? I understand it's a real challenge."

Stop! He'll suspect you're the eavesdropping neighbor!

Mordy stood, his jaw tense. "Please excuse me, Mrs. Weiner. I have some studying to do."

He's figured out it's her.

"Mordy, do you want some pecan pie before you leave?" Devoiry asked.

"No, Ima. I'm good. I *bentched*. I'm going to Shmueli's now. We're going to learn." He took his winter parka off the coat hook hanging by the front door and slipped his arms into the sleeves.

Mrs. Weiner sat a bit straighter at the mention of Shmueli's name.

"That's Shmueli Firestone?" she asked. "Such a nice boy. I knew his grandmother for many years. Fine family, a wonderful *chavrusa* for you," said Mrs. Weiner. "So, how's Shmueli doing in high school? I hear that Gemara is quite challenging for him."

Mrs. Weiner, why don't you just take out a bill-board?

Mordy's voice turned cold. "Shmueli is doing just fine in high school, and, so am I." He left the table. "Good Shabbos, Tatty, good Shabbos, Ima, good Shabbos, Mr. Weiss," he called out as he opened the front door to leave.

"Good Shabbos. I'll see you at *minchah*," answered Yossi.

First Jessica storms out, now Mordy. What's next?

Devoiry went to the kitchen and in a few minutes returned to the table with a decadent, glazed chocolate pecan pie and a server in hand. "Mrs. Weiner, you've met Mr. Weiss before."

"Mrs. Weiner, nice to see you again," he said cordially.

"Good Shabbos, Mr. Weiss. Actually, besides wanting to be sure that everything was all right with that young lady who drove off in such a tizzy,

I also walked over because I have something very important to discuss regarding you, Mr. Weiss."

Oy. This can't be good.

"Mrs. Weiner, may I slice you some pie?" Devoiry asked, placing the silver-handled server under a gooey slice.

"Gladly, my dear. At my age, you can finally stop worrying about calories," she said. Devoiry groaned inwardly. *If I were as slim as she is I also wouldn't have to worry about calories.*

Mr. Weiss took a bite and closed his eyes as he slowly chewed. "Hmmmm, you can sure make a pecan pie! Most of the ones I've tasted are just sickeningly sweet, but this is divine, the combination of the chocolate and the pecan — phenomenal!"

"Thanks. Secret ingredient: I'll never tell!" She smiled to herself. *Three tablespoons of brandy makes all the difference.*

"So, Mrs. Weiner, how can I help you?" asked Mr. Weiss.

She leaned forward, a smirk turning up the corners of her mouth. "Ah, it's how I can help *you* that brings me here!"

Mr. Weiss sat back in his chair. "Really? How's that?"

Mrs. Weiner dabbed the corners of her mouth with the cloth napkin, returning it to her lap, and cleared her throat. "Perhaps the Rosenbergs told you about our very confusing phone problem?"

"No. What problem?"

Trouble's coming.

"Well, I'm old enough to remember when phone lines used to be party lines, and it seems we've got one now. When I call the Rosenbergs, if they're speaking on the phone, it's not that I want to eavesdrop, *chas v'shalom,* but I can't help myself. I hear every word of their conversation," she declared.

Oh, no. What did she hear now?

"The phone company is coming Thursday to fix the problem," Devoiry said.

"Yes, I know, but I have to tell you, I think the whole mess-up is straight from Hashem. Wait till I tell you what I overheard. It's *gam zu l'tovah*!"

Yossi held his hand in midair before taking the next forkful of pie. "We're not speaking *lashon hara,* Mrs. Weiner, especially on Shabbos!"

"Of course not! No *lashon hara* at all. I'm just saying...perhaps you, Mr. Weiss..." she fixed her gray eyes on him "...have a problem, and I can help you solve it."

"Really, now. What problem do I have?" he asked.

"What did you hear, Mrs. Weiner?" asked Devoiry tersely. "Are you sure this is Shabbos talk?"

"Our Sages say that after Hashem created the

world, He busied himself with making *shidduchim*. So this is *definitely* Shabbos talk," replied Mrs. Weiner, with that cat-that-swallowed-the-canary look on her face.

"*Shidduchim?* Pertaining to me?" asked Mr. Weiss.

Mrs. Weiner took a bite of pie, chewing daintily, looking like she was relishing the attention. "Mr. Weiss, you're a widower. I understand you. I also lost my beloved Harold only three years ago. It's a terrible thing, being so alone, especially on Shabbos. I won't tell you how old I am, but I'm too old for a new husband. You, however, are still a young man. I understand you'd like to remarry, and I know just the woman for you."

Mr. Weiss raised his eyebrows. "Really, and how do you know what I'm looking for in a *shidduch*, Mrs. Weiner? We really don't know each other."

"Exactly, but I heard —"

"You were listening to my conversation about Mr. Weiss?" Devoiry asked, her voice rising. *How dare you, you meddler! Now I know how Mordy felt!*

Mrs. Weiner nodded, and looked at Devoiry. "On Thursday night, I called you to see if you were interested in making a donation to the Lancaster Hatzolah. You know, I help them raise money from time to time, and you were on the phone, and I was going to hang up right away of course because I'm *not* the eavesdropping type, but I just couldn't help myself when I heard you mentioning to your friend Susie that your efforts to find a *shidduch* for Mr. Weiss were not working. I couldn't help overhearing all the wonderful things you were saying about Mr. Weiss to your friend, so I had it in mind when —"

"When what?" asked Mr. Weiss, looking more troubled than delighted at Mrs. Weiner's intrusion into his private life.

"I have just the woman for you, Mr. Weiss. I have a feeling in my *kishkes* that she's just what you're looking for!"

Devoiry dropped her fork, causing a loud "ching" as it bounced off the plate. "Mrs. Weiner, I…I don't know what to say. Mr. Weiss, I apologize for this. This is not the way we'd normally be *redting* you a *shidduch*. I had no idea…"

Mr. Weiss chuckled. "I understand."

Mrs. Weiner straightened in her chair and paused for effect. She took another bite of pie, dabbed her lips, and took a prolonged sip of the tea Devoiry had served her.

"Mrs. Weiner, you're keeping us in suspense. Who is this wonder woman?" asked Yossi.

She placed her fork down on her plate, and pushed aside a half-eaten slice. For all that chewing, she'd barely made a dent in it. "Devoiry, your pie is delicious."

"Thank you," she murmured through clenched teeth.

"I'll tell you. I play mahjongg with the ladies every Friday morning. Gets our minds off the fact that it doesn't take us long to get ready for Shabbos anymore. I have a cleaning lady, I'm usually invited out for meals, so what's there to do? Anyway, we're chatting, and Mrs. Fryberger starts telling me about how her daughter Zahava Frankel needs a husband. And, I remember Devoiry telling her friend Susie that there's this Mr. Weiss — a widower, *frum*, settled financially, a gentleman — looking for a companion in his later years. I even remember, if I heard correctly, that Mr. Weiss is seeking a well-educated woman who likes to travel."

Mr. Weiss looked embarrassed from the succinct summary of his bio, recited aloud. "Mrs. Rosenberg got it right. But there's more to me than a few sentences. The Rosenbergs have known me for years. You really don't know me at all, Mrs. Weiner."

"Oh, but wait till you hear. This Zahava sounds just right for you — *more* than fits the bill. So my friend Mrs. Fryberger starts telling me that her daughter Zahava has been, tsk, tsk, a widow for many years. Her husband died when her daughter, Tzippy, was only thirteen, and she's raised her all alone."

"Tzippy? That's her granddaughter's name? That was my late wife's nickname, too," Mr. Weiss said somberly.

"It's a sign!" she exclaimed, her hands thrust into the air. "And you haven't heard the best part yet!"

"*Nu?*" asked Devoiry. *Get on with it already!*

"This Zahava owns her own business, and in a million years you won't imagine what she does. Okay, I'll tell you...She runs a travel agency!"

The tea Devoiry was drinking dribbled down her chin. As she snatched a napkin to wipe up the mess, she caught a slight smile on Mr. Weiss's face. *He does love to travel. Wouldn't that be amazing?*

"Where does this Zahava live?" asked Mr. Weiss.

"She lives in Baltimore, less than an hour and a half away! I told Mrs. Fryberger everything I knew about you. Zahava is in town now visiting her mother for a week — Mrs. Fryberger isn't in such good shape, so Zahava comes up from time to time to care for her.

"Anyway, I didn't get to meet her, because Zahava spends a lot of time at the local library with her computer so she can still conduct her business during the day — you know how it is. People who travel, they have no patience — they want it now. But I have seen pictures of her all over Mrs. Fryberger's house, and let me tell you, she looks great! Mrs. Weiner peered over her bifocals at Mr. Weiss. "So, *nu*, Mr. Weiss, why don't you meet her?"

Mr. Weiss stroked his long gray beard and smoothed out his *bekesha* as Devoiry anxiously awaited his response. Would he be open to this haphazard meddling by Mrs. Weiner? Could this actually be *bashert?*

Mr. Weiss picked up a homemade chocolate chip cookie from the table and savored his first bite. "You said this woman lives in Baltimore?"

"Yes, but she's visiting in Lancaster right now!"

"Mrs. Weiner, with all due respect to your efforts, you know that I run a wine and liquor business here in Lancaster, where I've been for many years. I've built up a fine business here that I wouldn't want to lose, and I'm not even remotely close to retirement. Sounds like this woman is planted in Baltimore with a business of her own. I'm sure neither one of us is prepared to uproot ourselves this late in life."

He stroked his beard again, looking thoughtful. His next words were spoken deliberately. "I also have to say that Yossi and Devoiry have worked very hard on my behalf, and it is true that certain *shidduchim* suggested haven't worked out thus far, but they know me very well, and they knew my late wife, and so I'm sure we must all just be patient, and in G-d's time, someone more well known to them or others who know me will surface. I'm not comfortable with this introduction coming out of the blue, from someone who does not know me or the woman being recommended. I beg your pardon, but I'm going to pass on this opportunity."

Mrs. Weiner slowly lifted herself out of her chair, grabbing her cane to steady herself. "Mr. Weiss, with all due respect, of course, I must tell you, I feel you are making a very big mistake. It is true that I do not know you, nor does Mrs. Fryberger. But Mr. Weiss, If the Ribbono shel Olam went through all the trouble of crossing the Rosenberg phone line with a busybody like me, don't you think it's worth making a phone call?"

Mrs. Weiner headed toward the front door. "Time for me to have my Shabbos nap. The older I get, the more I need one. I've done what I came here to do."

Devoiry got up to fetch Mrs. Weiner's coat. As she guided Mrs. Weiner's arm into the sleeve, the older woman steadied herself by holding on to Devoiry's lapel. "Dear," Mrs. Weiner said, her voice now the soft, trembling one of a fatigued elderly woman, "no sense being alone if you don't have to be. Believe me, Mr. Weiss doesn't want to end up like me, in his eighties, looking out the window half the day, hoping to see something to talk about."

Mrs. Weiner extended her arm through the second sleeve and then pulled her fur coat tight around her frail body. She looked ancient, much older than her years. *Loneliness is a terrible thing,* Devoiry thought.

Mrs. Weiner put one foot out the door and steadied herself with her cane. "My dear, when you get to be my age, you see that good can come out of just about anything, if you're willing to look for it — even those crossed phone lines of ours."

"*Gam zu l'tovah*," said Devoiry.

"Now if I could just figure out what's supposed to be good about this old hip of mine acting up," she complained as she hobbled down the walkway.

"Try giving up the heels, Mrs. Weiner."

Mrs. Weiner turned around to face Devoiry. "My dear, my face is all wrinkled, my back is bent over, I've got varicose veins in places I never knew there were veins! But on Shabbos, I'll be darned if I'm going out in public looking like a shmatte!

Seven

"OKAY, KIDS," YOSSI CALLED OUT as he steered the car onto the street where the kosher Chinese restaurant was situated. "Time to put your shoes on. We'll be there in just a minute."

"Yay, yippee!" Naftali and Malka chorused. Bracha was tuned in to the Miami Boys' Choir on her iPod, oblivious to the chatter of the younger children, and Mordy was learning in the back of the minivan.

Devoiry pulled down the lighted mirror on the visor and examined her *sheitel,* making sure that its blond curls were not unruly and her hair was completely covered. *You'd never know it's four years old. Yossi's right. Why waste money on a new one when we can keep making this one work?*

Devoiry turned back and smiled at the kids. "I know you're excited. Remember, your best behavior or we're not coming back here ever again!"

Yossi parked the car and the kids clambered out.

"Tatty, we almost never go out for dinner. This is great!" shouted Naftali, jumping up and down like a jumping bean.

Yossi high-fived him as they walked in the front door of the restaurant.

A maître d' wearing a Brooks Brothers black pin-stripe suit greeted them in the foyer.

"Reservation for Rosenberg," Yossi said.

"It's my eleventh birthday!" squeaked Malka.

The maître d' bowed to her. "Happy birthday, madam. May I show you to your seat?"

Malka giggled. "Yes, follow me, everyone!"

So nice to see Malka relaxed and happy. Get her away from school and she's a different child.

It was only a moment after being seated that a waiter dressed in starched white uniform was at Yossi's side. "May I show you a wine list, sir?"

"Ah, no, that won't be necessary. Just the regular menu will be fine. Do you have any specials tonight? How 'bout children's meals?"

"Well, sir, children twelve and younger can order from the children's menu, and I understand we have a special birthday girl tonight, so for her, it's on the house!"

"Tatty, what does that mean?" Malka looked up from the menu, her neck suddenly going into a spasm. "I can order anything I want? I don't have to worry about...?"

The waiter interrupted. "Not anything. Anything you order from the children's menu is on us. The rest is on your daddy. I'll be back in a few moments to take your order."

Malka's lips dropped into a pout, and she started blinking her eyes fast and squeezing her eyebrows together.

"Tatty," Malka asked, a whine creeping into her voice, "since it's my birthday and Mommy won the big prize, can I please, please, please, just get anything I want, just this once, without having to worry about whether it costs too much? Please?" Malka's neck jerked to the right. "Just this once?"

Give it to her, please, Yossi. Look how tense this is making her.

"Malka, I would also like to order whatever I want. But have you looked at the prices of this place? Sorry, sweetie, but you can order anything you want from the children's menu," Yossi said.

Number one rule of shalom bayis: don't argue in front of the kids.

"But Tatty, I don't want anything there!" Malka opened up the menu and started ticking off the items on the children's menu: "Chicken nuggets — yuck."

"Nuggets aren't yuck. That's what I'm getting!" shouted Naftali.

Devoiry scanned the menu. "They have hot dogs in wanton wrappers."

Malka crossed her arms. "Gross."

"How about chicken lo mein?" she tried again.

Malka's face twitched. "Ew, too many vegetables. And fried rice — no way. *Please*, Tatty, will you let me order something I really want? Just this once?"

Devoiry leaned to her right and spoke softly to Yossi. "Most of this dinner is paid for. It's her birthday!"

Yossi glared at Devoiry, and his voice was tense as he spoke to the entire table, not just to her. "Ima, the restaurant is offering Malka a free meal, and that's very generous of them, and we're not going to be ungrateful about it, now are we, Malka?"

Malka sulked for a second, but then surrendered. "Okay, but will you let me get my very own Coke in a can?" she begged.

"Certainly. Now everyone, here's the score. We have Mom's award money — thank you, Ima — and that's $150, and there's six of us here, but Malka goes free, so it's $150 dollars divided by five — we can each spend about $20 with tax and tip and drinks and so forth. So keep your eyes on the entrées that are $20 or less, okay? That's no problem for Tully, because his is on the children's menu. We'll have enough money left over to get ourselves a nice dessert to celebrate Malka's birthday."

"Tatty," Devoiry said, clearing her throat and pausing. *I hope he doesn't get mad at me.* "Do you think it's possible that this once, we could all just relax a bit about what everything costs? Since we got the gift money and all? Even if we went a bit over, it's not like it's all coming out of our pockets." Devoiry fiddled with her chopsticks, keeping her eyes away from Yossi. Then she looked directly at him, willing her voice not to tremble. "What do you think?"

Yossi's cold eyes told her exactly what he thought. "Ima, I'd appreciate it if you'd let me handle this. No reason we can't enjoy a wonderful meal and still keep ourselves within the family budget. Right, kids?"

"Whatever," mumbled Bracha. "I'm not even hungry. I don't know why we drove all this way just to go out to eat. We could have eaten in the Chinese restaurant close to our house, same thing! Mom could have made one of her fancy cakes, we could all sing happy birthday at home!"

Devoiry pasted a smile on her face, trying to diffuse the tension at the table. *This was supposed to be fun.* "Okay, everyone, look at this delicious menu. What's everyone going to order?"

The tenseness of the moment was gradually transformed into excitement as each child debated and negotiated with others to go splits, share, trade, and so forth, until finally everyone was ready to order.

Yossi called over the waiter and carefully spelled out each request. Then he said to the waiter, "Look, while our food is cooking, could you please send over the owner or manager? Is he in tonight?"

"Yes, sir," the waiter responded. "Is there a problem?"

"Not at all. We look forward to a delicious meal. It's just that I'm a businessman, and I think he'd like to hear what I have to say. I can help him make a lot more money."

Oh, no, not tonight. Can't you turn it off? Please don't ruin Malka's birthday celebration.

Devoiry felt sick to her stomach. She looked around the table to see if any of the kids had noticed. They seemed clueless.

"Let me see if I can find him, sir," the waiter replied.

I can't give him my "Don't do that!" stare because I'm sitting next to him.

As sweetly as possible, she asked, "What are you up to, Yossi?"

Yossi smiled, looking excited. "It's hard these days to make a profit. I'm sure he'll be anxious to hear what I have to say. Don't worry; it will only take a few minutes. I won't ruin anyone's fun."

Devoiry took a quick look around the table. Everyone looked eager and happy.

Hopefully this will just slide right by them, as long as they get their food.

In a few moments, a gray-haired, portly gentleman of about fifty, clean-shaven, with thick, black-framed eyeglasses strode over to their table from the kitchen with the confident steps of a successful business owner,. He reached out his hand to shake Yossi's. "Mr. Rosenberg, I'm the owner, Mr. Teitelbaum. Thanks for coming down tonight. I understand you've got a birthday to celebrate. Who's the lucky one?"

Malka raised her hand. "Me! Me! I'm eleven years old today!"

"Well, you look at least twelve to me. Just another year till your bas mitzvah! I hope you enjoy your special dinner."

"Oh, I will, don't worry. We never get to go out to eat. My daddy doesn't like to spend the money!"

Yossi tensed, but Mr. Teitelbaum laughed. "Well, we'll just have to change your daddy's mind about that, won't we? So," turning to Yossi, he asked, "Mr. Rosenberg, is there a problem? You wanted to see me?"

"No problem at all. We drove all the way from Lancaster to enjoy your fine restaurant. When we were here a year ago, the kids couldn't stop talking about how delicious the food was."

"Yeah, I *love* your egg rolls!" piped in Naftali.

"And you make the best fried rice I've ever tasted," added Devoiry. "I've tried to recreate the same taste in my own kitchen, and it never comes out the same."

"Trade secret," Mr. Teitelbaum joked. "So, Mr. Rosenberg, what can I do for you?"

Yossi pointed to the empty table next to them. "Mr. Teitelbaum, it's not what you can do for me, but what I can do for you. Have a seat for a moment."

Devoiry groaned inwardly and looked down at her plate. *Yossi, you sound like a used car salesman!*

Mr. Teitelbaum looked confused. "Well, Mr. Rosenberg, it's a busy night, but I can spare a moment."

Yossi pointed to the ceiling. "I couldn't help noticing your lighting. If I could save you a few hundred dollars a month on your electric bill, and it wouldn't cost you a dime, would you be interested?"

He nodded. "Sure! But there's no such thing as a free lunch — I've learned that in this business."

Yossi pulled out a business card from his wallet. "I run a business, Expense Reduction Associates. I specialize in helping business owners like you who have a lot of expenses that cut into their profit line. You pay me only out of what I save you, so it's basically cost free to you."

"With all due respect, what do you know about

the restaurant business?" Mr. Teitelbaum asked, sounding annoyed.

Devoiry wanted to crawl under the table, pretend that she didn't even know this man. "Yossi," she hissed, but he ignored her. He was just getting warmed up.

"Okay, see those lightbulbs? Hundreds of incandescent lightbulbs throughout your place. If you replace them with LED lightbulbs, your lighting bill will go down by almost 90 percent, and you'll be kinder to the environment. Buy the bulbs on ninety-day terms and they'll pay for themselves in just 195 days. They'll last six years if they're on twelve hours a day! I can get you those bulbs at nearly wholesale cost."

Mr. Teitelbaum didn't move to stop Yossi. "And I don't have to pay you anything for this?"

Yossi grinned. "Nothing out of your pocket. I take 25 percent of whatever I save you for the first two years, that's it. Want more?"

"Sure!"

Yossi nodded at the children's beverages around the table. "I see that the waiter brought my kids their Cokes and Snapples in individual cans and bottles."

Malka snatched her can of Coke and held it to her chest. "You can't take my Coke away from me, Tatty!"

"No worries, sweetheart. I'm just talking with Mr. Teitelbaum.

"But it's my *birthday,* Tatty, and all you *ever* do is work. Can't you for once not talk about your business?" Malka complained.

"I second that!" added Bracha.

"I third that!" chimed in Naftali, even though he really didn't know what he was saying.

Yossi cleared his throat. "Kids, just be patient. It'll only take a moment. I'm sure you'll be very happy for Mr. Teitelbaum when I show him how much money I can save him."

Devoiry felt the heat rising in her face. She put her index finger into her drinking water and trick-led some cold water on her forehead.

Yossi continued. "Mr. Teitelbaum, do you real-ize how much money you could save if you served drinks, with ice, in glasses, instead of individual servings like that? I can put you in touch with a guy who will give you kosher soda syrup at a frac-tion of the cost."

Bracha was fidgeting and she had an impatient look in her eye.

I know, Bracha. This has to stop.

"Yossi," Devoiry interrupted, "I'm sure Mr. Teitelbaum is very busy. Perhaps you can catch up with him on a workday?" *You're like a train speeding down the tracks and I can't stop you.*

"My wife is correct," said Yossi. "This might not be a good time for you. Want me to call you from my office?"

"You've piqued my interest, Mr. Rosenberg." He leaned in Yossi's direction. "What else have you noticed?"

Maybe I'll spill my glass of water all over his lap. That'll stop him cold.

Yossi looked at his family assembled at the large round table. "Kids, tell me, how many of you are going to eat with chopsticks tonight?"

Bracha raised her hand. Then Naftali's hand shot up to mimic her.

Can't stop him, might as well join him. "I've been enjoying Chinese food all my life, but I've never figured out how to use those things without the food spilling in my lap!" *So he can get chopsticks cheap, too? What doesn't he do!*

"Okay," Yossi continued, "so maybe three of us will use chopsticks, but you brought them out to the table for everyone. They look lovely, add to the atmosphere perhaps, but why not let the customers request chopsticks if they desire?"

"We do spend a lot of money on chopsticks. Have you a connection for those, too?" Mr. Teitelbaum joked.

Yossi lifted up his cellophane-wrapped chopstick and stared at it. "Well, actually, I do. I know a guy in restaurant supplies — and that includes chopsticks — who has the best prices I've seen."

Mr. Teitelbaum stood. "I really should get back to the kitchen. You've definitely caught my interest. Anything else before I go?"

Devoiry scanned Mr. Teitelbaum's face, looking for annoyance, but actually he looked intrigued. *Yossi has a gift for this. I should be proud, but right now I want to go home and give him a piece of my mind in private, away from the kids.*

Yossi pointed to the waiter nearby.

"Tatty, when are we going to *eat?*" Naftali whined. I'm *so* hungry, I could eat this napkin!" For effect, he stuffed the corner of it into his mouth.

"Tully, I'm sure they're going to bring the egg rolls in just a minute." Devoiry said. "Take that out of your mouth!"

Mr. Teitelbaum turned toward Naftali. "I promise you, those egg rolls are worth waiting for. If they aren't, you tell me, okay?"

"Okay!"

"Mr. Rosenberg, something about my wait staff?" he inquired.

"Yes, I noticed that your wait staff wears white. I'll bet you spend a fortune on laundry bills. Would you like to know how I could save you a bundle on your uniform cleaning?"

"That's it. Sold!" Mr. Teitelbaum stuck out his hand to shake Yossi's. "You have my interest, and respect! It really won't cost me anything?"

Yossi nodded. "I'm paid only out of what I save you in expenses. I've saved many business owners like you thousands of dollars, and there's no downside for you whatsoever."

Mr. Teitelbaum nodded. "Very impressive. Give me a call during the week. I'd like to pursue this. I'm hard to reach, but keep at it. It was a pleasure to meet you and your family. Enjoy the meal!"

Finally. Yossi, I've had enough. We can't continue like this anymore. You're possessed.

Mr. Teitelbaum looked directly at Naftali. "Pay attention in school. You'll end up smart like your daddy."

Naftali grinned. "I'm already smart. I got 104, top mark, on my spelling test!"

Mr. Teitelbaum laughed. "What's your name?"

"Naftali, but people call me Tully."

"Tully, how do you spell 'free dinner'?"

"Ah... F-R-E-E SPACE D-I-N-E-R?"

"Close enough. Tell you what, Tully. Just because your daddy is so smart, I have a special surprise." He turned back toward Yossi. "Mr. Rosenberg, I'm a cost-cutting kind of guy myself. So, I'm cutting your costs. Dinner's on me tonight!"

The kids erupted in yahoos and Malka asked, "Does this mean we can order extra dessert?"

"*Baruch Hashem!*" Devoiry exclaimed. "That's very kind of you, Mr. Teitelbaum. You didn't have to do that."

So much for me giving Yossi a hard time! Now he'll never see it my way.

"It's my pleasure. Looks like your husband is

going to save me enough money that I can afford it!" He laughed as he strode away.

Yossi sat back in his chair with the satisfied, demure smile of a man who had just accomplished something meaningful.

"Good job, Tatty. You were amazing!" Devoiry said, intentionally not looking anywhere near him. *What I really wanted was to spend just one hour with your undivided attention enjoying Malka's birthday.*

"Hey, Dad, you were really sharp. I've got to learn a few of those skills from you," said Mordy.

"Son, it all starts in here," Yossi said as he pointed to his chest. "You have to really believe in what you're doing."

"And that you do!" Devoiry said.

"Hey, Ima, now that Mr. Teitelbaum comped the whole meal, you can get that new Cuisinart food processor you've been wanting," Yossi said. "Would sure make your life easier in the kitchen!"

Now how am I supposed to stay mad at you?

Eight

"GIVE ME A BREAK, YOSSI. It's forty-two cents. Do you hear me?" Devoiry said. "You can't even buy a candy bar anymore for that, so please, stop making me feel so bad about this."

"Okay, what I did was dumb. Silly, moronic. But don't you find it even a little bit funny?" Devoiry asked from the passenger side of their minivan as she and Yossi set out for their appointment with the girls' school principal.

Devoiry started biting the fingernail of her index finger, a habit she resorted to only when she was fighting with Yossi.

Yossi was somber. "Frankly, I don't find the subject of wasting money even a little bit funny. And what I find the most disturbing is not that you wasted the money, but that you don't care! So what's forty-two cents? And then, what's forty-two dollars? And then, oh, well, so what's four hundred and two dollars? Where does it stop?"

"I make my own money, too, and if I wasted forty-two cents, well, I'll just take the loss!" retorted Devoiry.

"Don't even get me started! Your cookbook isn't selling and you're spending a lot more money on the groceries you buy for your recipes than we're making off the sales, so don't try that tactic with me!"

Devoiry looked out the window at the passing farmland, willing herself not to cry. *I hate the way I start to cry whenever I get really mad at Yossi!*

Even in the wintertime, the expansive farmland with acres of green fields, silos, and silhouettes of Amish farmers infused her with serenity, and she breathed deeply, hoping to extract from the scenery the peace she wanted to feel.

Yossi banged his fist against the steering wheel. "You know, Devoiry, I can't stand the way you always make me out to be the bad guy, like I'm some fool who is so cheap, you should have your head examined for being married to me. Why do I have to apologize for the fact that *yes,* even forty-two cents matters to me!"

Yossi paused, staring straight at the road, not looking at Devoiry. "Ever hear the expression

'Every penny counts'? Well, it's true! Have you or I ever been really, really hungry? Not the fasting-on-Yom-Kippur kind of hungry, with a smorgasbord at the end of the twenty-six hours. I mean, so ravenous, so emaciated from starvation, forty-two cents could make the difference between life or death?"

Devoiry cringed at the image.

"No, thank G-d, we haven't ever suffered like this!" Yossi continued, his knuckles turning white on the steering wheel. "But my grandmother starved to death in Auschwitz, and if she could have taken forty-two pennies and traded it in for a soft roll, or a couple of sucking candies, or a fresh apple, do you know what that would have meant to her?"

Devoiry was frightened of escalating the fight by responding. She allowed silence, as uncomfortable as it was, to be a passenger in the car. Finally, she found the courage to speak in a voice barely audible above the engine's humming noise.

"Yossi, I never thought of it that way. I'm sorry. I just laughed off my stupid mistake, didn't even think of the forty-two-cent stamp as anything real." Devoiry twisted her hands in her lap and fingered the buttons on her coat. "The truth is, you've taken such good care of our family, forty-two cents has never had to matter. I know you have really strong feelings about this, but you just have to lighten up.

You're wrecking our *shalom bayis* over — yes, I'm going to say this — a measly handful of coins. Is it really worth it? We're going to end up paying a fortune for marriage counseling if you don't cut it out!"

As a tear trickled down her cheek, Devoiry sniffled and reached for a tissue in her purse. *Oh, no, here I go again. I can't stand crying when I'm mad. Wish I'd keep the crying for the onions.*

Yossi glanced sideways at Devoiry, taking his eyes off the road only for a second, because he was always a cautious, responsible driver.

"Geez, I didn't mean to make you cry, especially now, when we're only five minutes from the school. You and I, we can really get worked up about this money thing, can't we?"

Devoiry nodded, the lump in her throat keeping her from talking.

"Tell me again how you managed to do this thing that cost us a postage stamp? Which of course makes me seem really ridiculous for giving you a hard time about it. I just want to understand."

Devoiry swallowed, the lump in her throat dissipating. She spoke softly, looking down at her feet. "Hadassah sent a pledge card, asking me to join the local Lancaster chapter. I wrote out a check, put it in an envelope, and mailed it to them." Devoiry's whisper turned into a slight giggle.

"But I was doing five things at once, so I put the check in the same envelope they used to mail the pledge card to me, stuck a new stamp on it..." Devoiry's giggle transformed into real laughter. "So then I mailed...the check right back...to myself. There I was, standing in the dining room opening the mail, and I opened the envelope addressed to me, hoping that it was a piece of fan mail or a check to order one of my cookbooks, something fun.... Well, geez, I thought you'd laugh with me, not get upset."

Yossi's mouth was turned up in the slightest of smiles, as he tried to maintain his serious composure, but ultimately failed.

Devoiry beamed at Yossi. "Come on, Yoss, *laugh with me*!"

Yossi steered the car into the parking lot, put the gears into park, and turned off the car engine. He took his hands off the steering wheel, then relaxed his body and turned toward Devoiry.

"Okay, you're right. I just got triggered. Sometimes I feel really alone, trying to conserve our resources, be a good steward. Seems like we're always battling about money, instead of being on the same side."

Devoiry adjusted her headband around her fall and applied some lipstick.

"I don't want to fight, even if you do drive me nutty now and then," she said, smiling. "We're good now, Yoss?"

"Sorry, Dev," said Yossi, shaking his head and looking chagrined. "Look, I don't mean to be impossible to live with and I don't want to fight with you."

Yossi reached for the door handle to get out of the car.

Devoiry got out of the car and walked over to Yossi. "Yossi, now remember, don't be too harsh about Malka when we're talking with her principal, Mrs. Goldstein. We don't want to give the impression that we're these 'Type A' parents who don't care about anything but good grades,"

"Yeah, I know," Yossi yawned, fatigued from a late night at the office followed by an early *shacharis* that morning. "Malka isn't Bracha. That's clear. Remember when we used to go to teacher conferences for Bracha and all we ever heard was *nachas*? A regular *nachas* machine."

"Don't compare them, Yossi. They're different people," chided Devoiry.

Yossi adjusted his *kippah,* more out of nervous habit than need. "This is a first for us, meeting with the principal about a problem with a kid. I'm kinda jittery. We've been so blessed with Mordy and Bracha. We were spoiled."

Devoiry's hands felt clammy inside her warm gloves. They walked toward the small brick building situated about ten minutes outside the city in Amish countryside. "Look, Yossi. I never get tired of the view from here. With all this farmland, you'd scarcely know that Lancaster is a city with millions of tourists visiting every year. Can you imagine a horse and buggy, and no heat in the wintertime?"

Yossi opened the heavy glass door and held it open for Devoiry to enter. "Actually, I think I would have made a very good Amish farmer. Few expenses, no waste."

They walked down the hallway to the principal's office. Karen, the front-office secretary, greeted them. "Hi, Mr. and Mrs. Rosenberg."

"Hi, Karen. How's your mom doing?" Devoiry inquired. "Is she out of the hospital yet?"

"*Baruch Hashem,* she's in rehab and doing quite well. Thanks for asking. Mrs. Goldstein is just finishing up a call. Please have a seat."

Devoiry and Yossi sat down on a couple of chairs crammed into an entryway cluttered with teacher paraphernalia, bulletin boards, a Xerox machine, and piles of books all over the tables, floor, and bookcases. Yossi pulled out his *gemara* and started to learn, while Devoiry fidgeted with the tassels on the end of her new designer-look-alike purse, compliments of the small consignment store in town she frequently visited.

"Mrs. Rosenberg, I bought your new cookbook," said Karen. "It's fabulous. I love all the gorgeous photos and the stories you write introducing each recipe. I have to confess though," she added, "that I don't really make your recipes. Good thing I don't cook as well as you do, or I'd be even heavier than I already am!"

"I know the feeling. It's always a battle, isn't it, keeping off those pounds," said Devoiry. *My size 10 probably doesn't look heavy to you, but it's a constant effort.* "May I ask you why you don't make any of my recipes?"

Karen's face flushed and her voice dropped to a half whisper. "I'm not much of a cook, certainly not a gourmet one, and my mom and I are on a limited budget. These gourmet ingredients are too expensive, and I'm afraid I'll spend all that money and turn out something inedible! I buy your book and put it on my shelf so people will think I cook gourmet," said Karen, laughing.

Devoiry bit her lip. *Oy. Maybe that's why my cookbook isn't selling. Too many Karens.*

"You realize, Karen, that if you ever had a question about a recipe, you could call me," she said. "The recipes are much easier than they look. You'd be surprised how many of these gourmet items you can find at Trader Joe's. I shop there all the time. Even the local Glatt Mart carries plenty of them. My recipes may look gourmet, but, believe me, they're easy."

Yossi, while concentrating on his learning, was tapping his foot on the floor.

"How long do you think it'll be?" asked Devoiry.

"She's off the phone now. Just one moment." Karen buzzed Mrs. Goldstein. "Mrs. Goldstein, the Rosenbergs are here to see you."

"Mr. and Mrs. Rosenberg, you can go in now."

Yossi closed his *gemara* and stood, followed by Devoiry, who walked behind him. Mrs. Goldstein, a modestly-dressed, petite woman sporting a short blond *sheitel* and a black suit, stood up from behind her desk as soon as they walked in, barely standing a foot taller than her massive desk, which was piled high with paperwork.

"Come in, come in and have a seat. So nice to see you both again. Please don't mind the mess," she apologized, pointing to stacks of papers all over the floor. "Somehow there's never any time for filing in this job."

She took her seat across from them at her desk. "I appreciate your taking time out of your busy schedules to come in during the day. Devorah, love your new cookbook. I made your brisket recipe for Shabbos, and it was really fabulous. No leftovers!"

"Thank you. I'm glad to hear that."

Mrs. Goldstein called the meeting to order. "Okay, let's get down to business," she said.

Nine

YOSSI DRUMMED HIS FINGERS AGAINST his *gemara*. "Let's get right to the point," said Yossi, taking the lead. "Malka is having trouble in her fifth-grade studies, we all know this. She's not like Bracha."

Mrs. Goldstein frowned. "We are enjoying both of your girls in our school, Mr. Rosenberg, and there's no sense comparing them, apples and oranges, each of them! It's true that Malka is having a bit of, shall we say, an 'anxiety problem,' and that's why I wanted to speak to you both."

Devoiry added, "Malka is generally a happy child, so it seems to be a problem with tests. Is that your understanding, too?" she asked, trying to soften her husband's male, get-right-to-the-point approach.

Mrs. Goldstein nodded. "It's true that Malka is a delightful girl. She brings so much life to the classroom. Her laugh really brightens up the room!"

"*Baruch Hashem,* all of our children are special. We're really fortunate," replied Devoiry.

"I've been speaking to Malka's Hebrew and English studies teachers, and it seems that Malka is a very bright girl, she asks all the right questions in class, pays attention, is very well-behaved, but as soon as —"

"When it's test-taking time, she bombs, right?" Yossi interrupted. "I've seen her test scores as of late, and they're terrible. That's not my girl! I mean, she's smarter than that. You can tell the difference between a student who tries hard and one who doesn't care, right?" he asked, adjusting his *kippah* on his head and fidgeting in his seat.

Mrs. Goldstein stood from behind her desk. "Let me show you both something I know you'll find interesting." She walked to the corner of the office where an old gray filing cabinet stood, four drawers high. She opened the second drawer and quickly put her fingers on the file she was searching for. Across the top in neat letters was typed, "Rosenberg, Malka."

"Uh-oh," said Yossi. "You have a file on my daughter, and something tells me it's not a *nachas* file."

Mrs. Goldstein turned to him with folder in

hand and said, "Oh, but it is! We started an experiment here with your daughter's teachers, and here are the results."

Experimenting on our daughter without our permission? How dare you!

Mrs. Goldstein removed the papers from the folder and laid them out across the desk. Devoiry spotted a smattering of test scores, ranging from 48 to 93, circled in red at the top.

Mrs. Goldstein picked up two tests, identical in content, Devoiry noticed, and one had 93 circled in red at the top, and the other, 57.

"Look at Malka's most recent science test. When she took it in class, this is the score she received." She pointed to the paper with the 57 on top.

"She came home crying that day! I felt so badly for her. She studied so hard for that test," Devoiry said.

"It's very upsetting to a child as smart as Malka to perform this badly on tests. So the next day, her science teacher told her that she could do a retake. This time, though, there was no time limit. Now here's what's fascinating..." Mrs. Goldstein's face lit up as if this were her first year as a Bais Yaakov principal instead of her fourteenth.

Yossi reached over and picked up the test with the 93 on top. "This was her second science test?"

"Yes," said Mrs. Goldstein, "and here's the interesting part. She took the exact amount of time for the second test. She knew the material cold, and she sailed right through the test. As long as she didn't feel panicked that she had a time limit, she did just fine."

Devoiry digested the news. "So you're telling us that Malka's teachers are willing to let her take tests untimed, and this could eliminate her anxiety?"

"It won't make the entire problem disappear like a magic wand, but it'll help us assess what she really knows. Look at her tests at the beginning of the year" — Mrs. Goldstein fanned out some of the tests across the desk — "and now look at the tests she took in the last week."

Yossi whistled. "I always knew my daughter was smarter than her grades." His face beamed with *nachas*.

"Mrs. Goldstein, that's really kind of you," Devoiry responded, brushing her hand through the bangs of her *sheitel*. "Malka hasn't mentioned anything to us. We had no idea about this new approach."

"I imagine that she didn't want you to know — she probably thinks of it as cheating. But I think of it as fairly testing her abilities. This is an easy enough accommodation for us to handle, especially if it gives us a more intelligent look at Malka's true understanding of the material."

"And the other kids in the class aren't jealous of her?" asked Devoiry. "I wouldn't want her classmates to resent her, like she's getting off easy or something."

Mrs. Goldstein rested her chin on her hand and thought about the question for a moment. "In my experience, generally speaking, the other children don't get jealous of accommodations we make for children who need it, because they are grateful that *they* don't need the accommodation!"

Yossi looked at his watch and then stood. "Thank you, Mrs. Goldstein. Very much appreciated. I'm sure it's time for you to get back to your busy job, and us, too. Thanks for keeping us updated. This is a great school, worth every dollar we pay for tuition, and more. Keep up the great work!"

"Mr. Rosenberg, please sit down. We're not finished here."

Yossi looked startled, and he sat down in his chair like a recalcitrant child. *It isn't easy to get Yossi to back down. The principal intimidates him.*

Mrs. Goldstein stared directly at Yossi. "Mr. Rosenberg, I've been a principal for many, many years. I want to caution you against a very common mistake that I've seen many more times than I care to count. Bracha, your oldest, is an outstanding student, really mature, smart as a whip, of the highest caliber. We're proud to have her as a student, and I'm sure she gives you much *nachas*."

Mrs. Goldstein leaned over her desk with a penetrating stare, and Yossi squirmed in his seat. "Your Malka is also a very special child. She'll never be Bracha, nor should she be. She's special enough in her own right."

Yossi cleared his throat. "Are you insinuating that we don't love our daughter, Mrs. Goldstein?"

"*Chas v'shalom!* But we can't ignore Malka's tics."

"Wait a minute!" Yossi's face flushed and he crossed his arms. "You're not suggesting that she has tics because of me? These spasms of hers come on all the time, even when I'm being superdad!" Devoiry wanted to say something, but how could she without getting in the middle?

Mrs. Goldstein waited a moment for the air to calm. Devoiry fingered her gold necklace, an intricate Jewish star and *chai* combined, inherited from Bubby Basha and a source of comfort for her, so she wore it often. "Mr. and Mrs. Rosenberg, your daughter Malka is presenting in the classroom as a troubled child. I believe that she's suffering, at least somewhat, from what we'll call 'older sister syndrome.' If you want your younger daughter to blossom, focus on her strengths, don't pressure her so much about her grades, and never use the words, 'your sister, Bracha —"

Yossi held up his hand, looking chagrined. "Guilty as charged. I'd hate to be in Malka's shoes. Bracha's shoes are too big. But really now, you're not suggesting that my daughter twitches her nose and jerks her neck around because I sometimes compare her to her sister?" He had that steel look in his eyes that Devoiry was so frightened by when he felt strongly about something, and no amount of reasonable conversation was going to budge him.

Mrs. Goldstein stood and walked behind her desk to the door. "Mr. Rosenberg, I had no intention of insulting you, *chas v'shalom*. I was merely suggesting that it's possible that Malka's tics might improve if everyone — that's you, and your wife, and her teachers, and even me — focuses on what we love about her, and how smart she is, and with a team effort, I think we can pull Malka through this crisis very nicely. It could be easier than you realize. Also, I can reassure you, from my experience, most children with these stress-related tics grow out of them by the time they get to high school."

"Thank you, Mrs. Goldstein, for taking such a personal interest in our Malka," Devoiry said. "Much appreciated."

"Are we finished?" Yossi asked with restrained politeness.

"I would like to check in with both of you in a couple week's time, after we've had a chance to see if this new system of test taking is working for Malka. I also suggest that you monitor her tics and notice whether they improve at all over the next few weeks. Okay?"

"Sure," Devoiry said as they both rose from their seats.

"Thank you for your time," Yossi said as they exited. "I hope I wasn't too difficult for you — it's not easy for me. I prefer the *nachas* meetings!"

"My pleasure. I really do adore your girls. You should consider this a *nachas* meeting," Mrs. Goldstein assured them.

As Devoiry and Yossi walked out of the office and headed back to the car, Yossi's cell phone rang and he became immediately absorbed in a business call. Devoiry's shoulders relaxed. *Good. That'll calm him right down.*

Devoiry signaled to Yossi that she'd drive home so that he could concentrate on the call, and he nodded his agreement. Devoiry rarely drove when Yossi was a passenger. He was so critical and she got so flustered — it was just easier to let him drive.

As she inched out of the parking lot, she looked in both directions more than once, careful to avoid any semblance of careless driving. She took her eyes off the wheel for a second to glance at Yossi, who was stroking his beard, his face animated, thoroughly engaged in conversation. She heard him say, "Mr. Teitelbaum." *Amazing. The restaurant owner from Baltimore called him.*

"Sure, I'll take a drive down. How's Wednesday this week? Morning, before you open? Yes, ten o'clock works fine. Before then, gather together an itemization of all your monthly expenses. Good place for us to start."

Cool. Maybe we'll even get some free meals out of it, too!

As she drove, a familiar mixture of emotions caught in her throat — admiration for her husband's business skill and appreciation for their high standard of living that resulted, together with an irritation that twisted her insides.

Yossi ended the call and turned to her, his face glowing. "Remember the Chinese restaurant? He's in! Not only does he want me to show him how to save money in that restaurant, but he's also going into partnership with another guy, opening up another upscale kosher restaurant in the near future, and he wants to get me involved on the ground floor — before they even build. Yahoo!" He punched the air with his fist, victorious in the first round.

"*Baruch Hashem*. Nice work, Yossi. I'm so glad to hear it! You really are good at what you do," said Devoiry.

"Careful, Dev," he warned. "Don't ride the bumper of the guy in front of us. Give him space!"

"Yossi, don't start up on me again. I've had my driver's license for twenty years. I know how to drive! Don't make me nervous."

He hooks me every time. Wish I could just ignore it.

"Dev, I just gotta ask you. Did it bother you at all that they're experimenting with our daughter? Without telling us first? It really bugs me."

"Oh, Yossi, it's not like they were doing anything that could hurt her. They're actually going out of their way to make her life easier, so let's be *dan l'kaf zechus*."

Yossi shrugged. "It really makes me mad when I feel that someone wasn't honest with me. Don't tell me after the fact, like I'm the last to know — that's not my way. I don't like surprises. But you know that, of course."

Devoiry felt a muscle spasm right under her shoulder blade, the first place in her body to signal tension. She hadn't told Yossi about Mordy and his confession that he cheated on that one paper. Mordy was taking care of it. He promised to do *teshuvah*. Should she tell Yossi or keep it private between her and Mordy? What if he hates being the last to know? What if Yossi finds out that she knew, and didn't tell him? Mrs. Weiner wouldn't mention anything to Yossi, would she?

"Dev, what's on your mind? You look tense. Hey, watch out for that light up ahead. Turns fast from yellow to red, sneaks up on ya. Meeting was okay with you?"

"Sure, yes," she said as she slowed to a stop at the light. "I'm actually grateful to Mrs. Goldstein for reaching out to help our Malka. No, it's not that..."

"What, then?"

"Um, well...just so you won't be surprised... Mordy is having just a bit of trouble in English at school, but don't worry, he's on top of it, turning it right around!" she assured him quickly.

"Trouble? I thought he was acing his classes, Hebrew and English?" Yossi's voice rose.

"Hebrew, for sure. Top of his class. English, well, doesn't come as easy to him, that's all. He has some trouble with his writing skills."

"Why haven't his teachers said anything? They seem quite pleased with his work. How'd you learn about this?" Yossi looked at the speedometer. "Careful, speed limit here is twenty-five miles per hour, as long as we're driving by that school, and you're going forty. The cops'll nab you and we'll be paying the ticket!"

Devoiry grimaced. *I can't deal with another blowup. One fight a day is more than my quota. I'll tell him just enough.*

"Yossi, you can be really proud of your son. His *middos* are spot-on. He was put in a tempting situation where he could have cheated and gotten away with it, but he felt so guilty, he's —

Yossi reacted like an ignited match. "What do you mean, he cheated? Our Mordy? A cheater?"

Devoiry's foot reflexively floored the gas as she reacted to his outburst. She slowed back down again, not wanting to get him further agitated.

"No, Yossi, that's the point. He's *not* a cheater. He got some extra help on a history paper, that's all, turned it in as his own, realized that this could be construed as cheating, came clean with the prof, and now he's rewriting the paper all by himself. Really, you can be proud, not mad. He's a good boy. Always has been."

Yossi collapsed back into his seat. "What's happening here, Dev? First I'm called in to meet with Malka's principal, and now you're telling me that Mordy's having trouble, too? Am I doing something wrong? Failing my kids, you, somehow?"

Devoiry allowed herself to glance his way for a moment, sorry to see the dejected look on his face. *Maybe I shouldn't have told him about Mordy.*

"Listen, Yossi, seems to me that this is a great opportunity for us both to look at the glass as half full. Our Malka's a smart girl with only a bit of test anxiety, and our Mordy is a real *masmid* who maybe needs a bit of English tutoring, but he's a *talmid chacham* in the making. Bracha can have a bit of an attitude, but we're just riding the waves of adolescence, and as you said before, she always gives us *nachas*. We're good, Yossi, really good. Let's be *b'simchah*!"

Yossi bit his lip and adjusted his *kippah* again. "You think I'm too hard on them? On you?" he asked.

Don't make nice. Be honest. Here's your chance.

But not while you're driving.

Devoiry pulled the car into the entrance to a public park and let the engine idle. She wanted to give this conversation her full attention. It was a long time coming. She turned to Yossi, who was looking at her anxiously.

"Oh, man, what's going on? This is serious enough that you gotta stop driving?"

"I don't want to drive while we're speaking about this. Listen, you mean well. I know you do. But sometimes...the forty-two cents, riding on Malka because she got a 78 on her science test, expecting Mordy to ace every subject...it's too much. We all tiptoe on eggshells around you, afraid to let you down. *Chas v'shalom,* we might waste something — a bad tomato, a spilled glass of milk — we hide it from you so you won't get mad. The kids are afraid of you sometimes."

"*Afraid of me?* Why? I'd never lay a hand on them!" he steamed, adjusting his necktie.

"Of course you wouldn't," her voice soothed him. "This isn't about physical safety. It's about... being real."

Yossi squinted his eyes and cocked his head, as if hearing her correctly would help him decipher the message better. "Come again?" he said.

Devoiry had waited fifteen years to gather the courage to say this to him. Her hands trembled and her heart banged in her chest, giving rise to such a forceful panic attack that she almost opened the car door for air. Again she fingered Bubby's necklace, drawing courage when she thought of her. "Yossi, here it is — straight up," she said, finding her voice. "Take your frugal, incredibly sharp business skills, your Ivy League standards for excellence, your dedication to making sure everything is under control to the office. At home, we all...need you to relax."

Yossi didn't respond, and Devoiry inhaled slowly, and then exhaled, resisting the temptation to fill in the silence with more babble.

"Dev, what happens when you don't follow a recipe precisely, like when it calls for four eggs, but you just throw in three, or it requires two tablespoons of yeast, but you don't have it on hand, so you put in only a tablespoon? How does it all turn out? Life needs *seder*. Precision has its place. Otherwise, we just have chaos."

Devoiry nodded. She understood where he was going. *He thinks if he follows a formula, keeps to the recipe, everything turns out better. Keep control, better outcome. Not always.*

"Yossi, sometimes I follow a recipe to the letter, and still, it bombs. Who knows why?" She shrugged. "I can't figure it out. Other times, I just follow my whims and turn out something everyone raves about, and I'm embarrassed, 'cause all I did was throw together a little of this, a little of that, and everyone wants to know how I did it. Recipes have their place, but there's also something to be said for my best hits — they're usually the ones I didn't plan, couldn't replicate, just created in some kind of relaxed way, or they're Bubby's recipes from long ago — simple, *heimish*, nothing complicated, a few good ingredients thrown together in a pot."

Yossi opened the window for some air, and Devoiry appreciated the brisk cold that suddenly filled the car. He stared out the window for a moment and then turned back. "Life *is* complicated, Dev. Raising four kids with enough money for yeshivah, the *chuppah*, setting them up, keeping them on the *derech*, trying to be a good husband, business owner, make the minyan, daven three times a day, all of it, a large heaping pile of responsibilities, from the second I open my eyes till my head hits the pillow at night. If I don't keep control —

"What, Yossi?" she asked softly. "What happens?"

He looked at her with a blank expression on his face. "I...don't...know..."

Ten

Devoiry heaved the last of the supermarket bags into the back of her minivan, counting to be double sure she had everything. "One box of cookbooks to sell. One, two bags from Glatt Mart. One, two, three bags from the Save-A-Lot grocery store. One, two bags of paper goods from the dollar store," she ticked off the items, comparing the stuffed bag against a master list she was carrying.

Yossi would be proud of me. I stayed on budget for supplies. He's been a little lighter in the house since our talk. Malka's tics seem to be better at home. Wonder if there's a correlation.

She slammed the back door shut, since the old car had a tendency to become unhinged while driving, and climbed into the driver's seat, ready to back out of the driveway, when she heard a horn honking and, turning, saw Jessica's car pulling up to the curb. She quickly opened her car door and stepped out as Jessica got out of her car.

"Jessica, it's so nice to see you again. You caught me just as I was leaving."

Jessica looked down at the ground, hesitating to meet Devoiry's gaze. "Uh, I came for my suitcase. But I can come some other time."

"It's no problem." Devoiry reached out to hug Jessica, feeling Jessica's back stiffen. "Sorry I don't have time to chat. The Agudah sisterhood hired me to do a cooking demo for their luncheon. I'm on my way over there. Let me just unlock the house and grab your suitcase for you."

"I would appreciate that. Thank you."

As they walked up to the front door, Devoiry stole a glance at her watch. *I need at least an hour to set up for this cooking demo. No time now to talk or I'll be late.*

Devoiry unlocked the door and invited Jessica to wait inside while she scampered upstairs. She regretted being unable to take the time to talk with Jessica at least. She'd been so worried about her, and she kept wondering what they could have done differently. A moment later she returned with the suitcase.

"Here ya go. It was wonderful having you," she said.

"Yeah, right," said Jessica as she fumbled for the suitcase handle. "Not exactly! Sorry I left so abruptly."

Devoiry ushered her out of the house while she relocked the door and they walked back to the car.

Jessica kicked a small pebble she found on the driveway. "I'm so embarrassed."

"We didn't mean to upset you. Please forgive us. We'd love to have you again."

"Thanks. I don't know..."

They'd reached Devoiry's car and Jessica made no move to leave.

What should I do? Be late for the demo? What's more important?

"Wow, Mrs. Rosenberg," she said, peering in through the window, "you've got a carful. You have to bring that much stuff with you?"

"I know, what was I thinking, agreeing to do all the shopping myself for the cooking demo! What a hassle. But all I need is to get there and find out that my designated shopper forgot the meat. So I prefer to take care of it myself."

"Kinda like when I show up for midterms with my own pencils! Only more so."

"Right. Listen, Jessica, I'd love to help you sort things out, and I promise, no pressure. Let's schedule a time that works for you, okay?"

Jessica looked up, her face tense, but with the

beginnings of a smile. "Not giving up on me yet, huh?"

"Never!" Devoiry gave her shoulder a squeeze. "I'm afraid you're stuck with the Rosenbergs for life, as long as you'll have us. And all our craziness!"

"Mrs. Rosenberg, your kind of crazy is what I've always wanted."

I should invite her to the cooking demo but I just can't. I'll worry the whole time about whether she's enjoying herself.

Jessica picked up her suitcase. "Okay then, um, winter break's next week. Maybe I could call you, you know, stop by, when it's good for you? I'm not going home. I don't really want to be around my family right now, till I sort things out."

Devoiry reached over and hugged her again, feeling Jessica hug her back this time. "Tell you what. I'm catering a small party a week from Sunday, and I would love some help in the kitchen. Can you take orders from a feisty, scatterbrained chef who has too much to do and not enough patience?"

Jessica relaxed and laughed. "Are you going to make me wear a skirt, or is this acceptable?" she asked, pointing to her well-worn jeans.

"Wear whatever you want. I'll even supply the apron. How's next Thursday work for you? For a Sunday gig, that's when I'll be doing a lot of my prep work. Say about ten or so? That way I can daven after the kids go off to school."

"Sounds good. I'll see you then. Thanks, Mrs. Rosenberg."

"You know, we're practically friends. You can call me Devoiry."

Jessica wrinkled her nose. "Doesn't sound right. Sorry. You'll always be Mrs. Rosenberg to me. You're kinda like my mom...only...not like her at all!"

Devoiry opened the door of her car and climbed up to the driver's seat. "Ewww, makes me sound so old. Well, as long as you don't call me 'ma'am.'"

"Yes, ma'am," Jessica teased as she turned and walked to her car, turning around once to wave.

She waited for Jessica to drive off and then headed down the driveway and the tree-lined street of her neighborhood.

What a sweetie. Baruch Hashem, all is not lost. Now on to the sisterhood luncheon.

Devoiry glanced at the car dashboard clock. It said 10:45. *Lunch starts at noon. I'd better skedaddle!*

Devoiry turned off the Avraham Fried CD she loved to listen to and used the five-minute drive to daven for a successful luncheon. She prayed for a good turnout, delicious food without any kitchen mishaps, and several cookbooks sold, the primary reason she agreed at all to do this very time-consuming and stressful gig, the hundred-dollar speaking fee not compensation enough for the hours spent shopping and setting up. *At least they reimburse me for the food,* she thought. Then she reviewed the menu in her mind: simple and healthy, make-at-home salad dressing with greens, beef stroganoff with mushroom brown rice, chicken breast in wine sauce, and chocolate crunchies for dessert.

They said I should plan on about twenty women. Do I have enough food? Jewish mother's syndrome. Wonder who'll show?

Devoiry pulled into the parking lot of the town's only Orthodox shul, a simple, rust-colored brick building with no windows. No one would know that it was a synagogue except for the name emblazoned on the front in simple silver gray letters, "Agudath Israel." A simple place to pray with a small, committed congregation of Jews who took their prayers very seriously. There was no stained glass or ornate architecture — which was exactly why Yossi loved to daven there.

Good thing they have a well-equipped kitchen.

She drove the car right up to the back door, close to the kitchen. *I'm not looking forward to shlepping all these bags and a case of cookbooks. Why didn't I bring a friend to help?*

She popped the trunk and got out of the car, re-securing the ponytail holder for her *sheitel* to keep any stray blond curls from dipping into the pot.

She gathered up a bag in the crook of each arm and shuffled over to the door, trying not to trip on her long skirt. With the pinky of her right hand, she grasped the door handle and opened it, clutching the bags to her chest.

Should've worn my flats. What was I thinking wearing heels?

"Hello, hello, anyone here?" she called out. "I could use some help."

The building was eerily quiet, and there was only one car in the parking lot, a Toyota Camry belonging to the rabbi, whom she didn't want to bother. Still, she hoped that the janitor might be around somewhere. Nelson had been a fixture in the shul for so many years, he was considered family.

She edged her way carefully with her load down the staircase and through the corridor into the social hall, where the kitchen was located at the back of the room. Her arms were aching from the load, and she had several more trips to make. She glanced at the wall clock, noting that the women would probably start arriving in forty-five minutes.

Too little time. Why didn't I come earlier?

"Hello, Mrs. Rosenberg," a voice called out. "Looks like you could use some help." Asher Levine, a lanky, awkward boy with a ravaging case of acne covering his cheeks and forehead, came forward to take her bags.

"Asher, you're a godsend. You learn here now during the days, right?"

"Yes, ma'am. Yeshivah didn't work out. I homeschool. I was in the *beis midrash* when I heard you yell. Want me to take the rest of your bags in for you?"

"Fantastic!"

"Asher, there's a box of cookbooks I need, too. Careful, they're heavy. It'll probably take you a few trips. Then you can lock up the car."

"No problem," he said as he strode out. *He must be so lonely. Such a nice boy. Baruch Hashem he was here.*

Devoiry had prepared many meals in this kitchen, because she was called on often to cater social functions for the Orthodox community, as small as it was. She knew the lay of the land and began quickly removing the contents of the shopping bags, placing them in an organized way around the *fleishig* kitchen according to the menu. She stopped for a moment to take stock.

It'll be crowded in here with all the ladies watching me cook. How many folding chairs do they have set up? 1, 2...4...10...12 chairs. I hope they're expecting more than 12! I bought food for 20. The rest will stand, I guess.

Asher showed up with the next load of bags and placed them on the counter.

"Mrs. Rosenberg, I've got one more trip, and

that'll do it. Want some help setting up?"

She nodded. "See those tables with the tablecloths outside the kitchen? We're expecting twenty for lunch, and I have all the paper goods. I would be so grateful if you'd help me set the tables while I prepare the food."

"Sure thing!" he grinned, revealing a missing front tooth, knocked out in a bicycle accident years ago and never replaced. "I'll be right back!" He hurried out of the room in a half skip, half run.

"You don't need to run, Asher. I don't want you to hurt yourself! And don't forget the box of books, okay?" she called out into the empty hallway.

If his family would accept tzedakah, I'd pay for him to get a new front tooth and a visit to a dermatologist. Wish his parents would let the community help them.

Nelson, a sturdy man of about thirty, popped in carrying a mop in his hand, trailed by a bucket of dirty water. "Be careful not to slip, missus. I just made the floor shine for your luncheon. Don't worry about the cleanup — I'll take care of it for you all."

"Great. Thanks so much!"

Devoiry glanced again at the wall clock, a knot forming just above her stomach. Time was marching faster than she was keeping up. Like a DVD on fast-forward, she removed the food from the shopping bags.

Good thing I washed all the vegetables. Okay, salad

greens, oil, spices, lemons for the dressing. Next, beef stroganoff. Got the rice already cooked, flour, the tofutti sour cream, mushrooms, onions, beef broth, where's the beef? Beef, beef, where are you? Must be in the bag Asher's bringing in. Take a deep breath. Chicken in wine sauce. Chicken cutlets, check. Broth, scallions, wine, garlic, onions, moving on to dessert. Chocolate chips? Got 'em, Trader Joe's dark, the best. Could use some chocolate now. Two bags, good. Double boiler. Take it out of the cabinet. Crunchy cereal? Here it is, so all I'm missing is the beef. That's weird.

Asher walked in with the last grocery bag resting on top of the box of books, and plopped them on the counter. "Whew, that was heavy!" he said, wiping sweat off his brow with his sleeve, despite the cold weather outside. "How many books do you have in there?"

"Nineteen now." Devoiry popped open the box and removed one of her cookbooks and handed it to him. "Here, Asher. Give this to your mom."

"Thanks. Ready for action! Want me to start setting the tables?"

"Hold on a minute." She quickly dumped out the contents of the remaining bags. Paper plates, napkins, and cups rolled all over the counter and she pawed through the piles. "That's strange," she said. "Where'd my pepper steak packages — five of them — go?" Her brow furrowed.

Devoiry's palms broke out in sweat and she felt

dizzy as she held onto the counter. "You okay, Mrs. Rosenberg?" asked Asher. "You look kinda sick."

"Just stressed. Can't locate my main ingredient, the beef. Maybe it's right in front of me. See it anywhere?"

Asher scanned the piles of food spilling all over the kitchen counters, looking carefully underneath each item. "No beef, Mrs. Rosenberg. None here."

Devoiry brightened. "Oh, I know, happens all the time when I shop. Would you be so kind and go back to the car, look in the trunk and backseat. Probably just slid out of the bag."

She handed her keys to Asher, feeling better already. *You know you bought the meat. Five pounds, paid a pretty penny for it. It's gotta be there. Don't sweat it.*

Devoiry gathered together all the paper goods and brought them out to the social hall. *Large plates for the entrée, bowls for the salad, forks, napkins, cups, check.*

Asher strode back into the room with a worried look. "Mrs. Rosenberg, sorry to tell you, but there's no meat in that car of yours. I checked it really careful. Nothing there but some old notebooks, candy bars, and some orange juice."

Devoiry collapsed into the closest seat, her heart racing. *Beef stroganoff — how do I make beef stroganoff without the beef? Did I leave it at Glatt Mart?*

"Mrs. Rosenberg, want me to start on the tables?" Asher asked.

"Ah, yes, tables, right, sure. Set for twenty, ten to a table, two tables, here's the stuff." She pointed to the pile of paper goods collected on one table, rubbing the temples of her forehead. *No, not a migraine. Not now.*

She glanced at the clock. *Do I have time to rush to Glatt? Thirty-five minutes till everyone will be arriving. Set up to do. Mushroom stroganoff, is that what I do? Oh, no, this can't be happening. What a nightmare. Where's the beef?*

Eleven

"Good afternoon, ladies. Welcome to the sisterhood cooking demo, with our very own Lancaster celebrity, Devoiry Rosenberg!" said Sarah Feist, Agudah Sisterhood president for so many years running, everyone assumed she'd hold the position until she was too old to remember her name.

"Most of us have already tasted her cooking, so we know we're in for a real treat. She's promised to show us a few secrets so we can at least *pretend* to be as good as *she* is in the kitchen!"

Please G-d, no one came today just to learn how to cook beef stroganoff.

"Sorry for the crowded conditions, standing room only, but we're here to watch the chef in action, so enjoy your seat if you have one, and if you're standing, I hope you wore comfortable shoes! Devoiry, ready?"

Devoiry inhaled deeply and put on her best, beefless, welcoming smile. "Sure am! Good afternoon, ladies. Thanks for coming. They expected about twenty for lunch and I see that about thirty of you showed up, but you know how it is, no matter how many guests show up, you can always slice the gefilte fish thinner!"

I don't recognize half the women in this room. Maybe I'll actually sell a few cookbooks!

Devoiry stood behind the kitchen island with her hands resting on the counter, and then she picked up a knife, ready to begin.

"Before we begin, I want to explain one change in the menu. You'll see that beef stroganoff and chicken in wine sauce were to be the main courses today. I have great news for those of you who are watching the calories — and aren't we all! My apologies, my beef seems to have run off on me, so I'll be introducing you to the début of a brand-new entrée, never seen or tasted before this day... chicken stroganoff! Now that the price of kosher beef has skyrocketed, my husband, Yossi, is always asking me to cut back on the beef, so won't your husbands be thrilled when you come home with a recipe for stroganoff that's half the price!"

This better work. I've never combined chicken and

pareve sour cream before. What if it's awful?

"You've got the recipe for chicken in wine sauce in your packets you can try at home — don't worry, it's easy. And where you see the recipe for beef stroganoff in your handout, substitute chicken breast instead. All right, ready to get started?

A chorus of yesses greeted her.

"First, you need a gigantic skillet, like this one, with a lid, and a good excuse to cry while you thinly slice a whole lot of onions. I had my good cry before I came here so I wouldn't ruin my makeup." She tilted a bowl full of sliced onions toward the ladies.

"Now, drizzle the olive oil into the pan, turn on the burner, and let those onions get started. Put the lid on to cook 'em up faster, and meanwhile, slice up a twelve-to-sixteen-ounce carton of mushrooms, any kind you like. You'll see I've got here baby bella mushrooms, my fave."

Heels are killin' me already. Why didn't I just dress comfy?

While the onions were sizzling, Devoiry sliced up the mushrooms with the speed of a professional chef.

"Wow, look at her go. I'd slice my fingers off if I tried that!" murmured an admirer from the crowd.

"She makes it look so easy. Wish I could cut that fast!" agreed another.

"Question for you," called out a woman from the back row, standing.

Devoiry looked up from her cutting board to see a tall, mid-fifties brunette with a navy blue suit offset by a purple and pink silk scarf tied elegantly around her neck.

Don't know her. Visitor?

"Of course, ask away while I chop."

"I see your menu today is quite caloric. Stroganoff with that fatty pareve cream sauce, chocolate for dessert — couldn't you just get rid of the cream sauce, and make something that isn't quite so dreadfully bad for your figure?"

Size six, if that. Lighten up, lady. Food is to be enjoyed.

"Of course, there's a time and place for that, but my attitude is, it's all about portion control. How disappointing would your Shabbos table be if you only served health food?"

"Shabbos calories don't count," said Devoiry's friend Susie.

Thanks, Suze.

Devoiry opened the lid of the skillet and slid the pile of sliced mushrooms into the pot. "You also want to add plenty of chopped garlic, to taste," she said, adding a dish of chopped garlic she'd prepared. The aroma of olive oil, onions, and garlic permeated the kitchen.

"I want to eat it now!" said Mrs. Weiner, waving

at her from a seated position next to a group of her friends.

Devoiry dabbed at her forehead with a nearby square of paper towel, the heat from the range starting to melt her makeup.

"I know what you mean. Add onions and garlic to anything, and it smells amazing," she said.

"Now, thanks to Tabatchnick, you can add a full quart of chicken broth right out of its container," she said, opening the carton of stock and adding it to the skillet, "but of course if you have your own homemade broth on hand, even better. Close up the lid, and let the broth heat up while you slice the chicken cutlets."

Devoiry took a chef's meat knife and deftly cut the chicken into slivers. "If you were making beef stroganoff, it's time to put the meat in."

Hope they won't be upset about the missing beef. I feel so stupid.

Now that we've sliced up these chicken cutlets, we'll get them into the broth to cook." She opened the lid and placed the pile of raw sliced chicken into the pot, replacing the lid.

Please, G-d, make it taste like beef stroganoff, only better. I'm winging it here.

"While that cooks till the chicken is tender, let's get dessert going." Devoiry washed her hands with soap in the sink. "Don't forget, ladies, always be careful when handling raw chicken."

Devoiry brought out the double boiler, poured water into the bottom, and put it on the fire. "Okay, ladies, here's an easy recipe to use up that high-fiber cereal you bought because it's healthy — you know, the one that looks like twigs, and tastes like it, too!"

She opened two bags of Trader Joe's chocolate chips and poured them into the top pot. "You're going to melt this chocolate all the way. Of course, you won't melt two full bags of chocolate chips when you're doing this at home."

"Speak for yourself!" said Bertha Finkelstein, a woman who made no pretense of ever being on a diet. "I can eat one of those bags in an evening!"

Devoiry laughed. "I know what you mean. I've had those days myself!"

"While the chocolate's melting, let's check on our chicken." She lifted the lid and the savory smell of chicken soup wafted through the crowded kitchen. The ladies reflexively inhaled the aroma.

"Hmmm, smells like Shabbos!" Devoiry said. "Woman standing in the back, you mentioned being health conscious. What's your name?"

"Zahava Frankel."

No kidding, it's Zahava! The shidduch for Mr. Weiss! What's she doing here? Mrs. Weiner was right — she looks amazing!

"You're new to Lancaster?"

"I'm visiting my mother, who was planning to

come today, so she brought me along."

Mrs. Fryberger, a frail woman in her nineties who made Mrs. Weiner look young, waved.

"That's terrific. So glad you could make it, Zahava."

Mr. Weiss told me that Mrs. Weiner wouldn't leave him alone about it, so he was going to call her. Wonder if they've spoken yet.

Devoiry stirred the contents of the pot, bringing her mind back to the comment she had been about to make. "Anyway, Zahava, you were worried about the cream sauce. So you can modify now and keep it out, but then you can't call it stroganoff. Ladies, see how this is too liquidy to serve as is?"

The women close by peered into the pot from their places.

"Throw in about a half cup of flour and then keep stirring till the flour is absorbed." Devoiry scooped out the flour with a measuring cup and tossed it into the pot.

"Suze, wanna help me out?"

Susie jumped out of her chair. "You bet. What should I do?"

Devoiry handed her the large *fleishig* spoon. "Keep on stirring gently till you feel the sauce thicken. Meanwhile, let's check on the chocolate chips."

Devoiry opened the lid and stirred the chocolate. "Perfect. All melted. Okay, I need another volunteer."

"I'll do it," Zahava volunteered from the back.

"Great! Come on over." *Let's see if the gal can cook. Mr. Weiss sure needs it.*

"Zahava, stand right here." She positioned her in front of a large bowl full of high-fiber cereal. *My goodness, this woman is tall. I'm only up to her shoulders. I feel like a pip-squeak!* She removed the pot of melted chocolate from the double boiler and rested it on a hot plate next to the cereal. "Here's what I want you to do. Take this bowl of cereal and pour it all into the liquid chocolate."

"All of it?"

Beautiful light blue eyes, expensive makeup. Mr. Weiss's type? Never. Too high-maintenance. He's looking for a heimish balabusta, like his first wife.

"Yes, go ahead. You'll see how it gets absorbed."

Devoiry took advantage of the moment for a closer look. *Real pearls, custom sheitel, expensive suit, looks like two-hundred-dollar pumps, and she has to already be five feet ten without them. On the outside, she's a great match for Mr. Weiss — he's always well dressed — but she's too pricey for him.*

"That's it. Stir till the cereal is completely mixed in." She turned toward the stove. How's the gravy now, Suze?"

"A lot thicker!"

"Okay, be right there. Zahava, here are a couple of large trays with parchment paper on the bottom." Devoiry looked out at the audience. "Don't forget the parchment, ladies. Makes cleanup a breeze. Zahava, take this spoon and scoop out a couple of tablespoons at a time and form chocolate clumps on the parchment. Trust me, it'll taste like gourmet candy when it's cold! *No one* will ever guess that the crunchy comes from cereal! By the way, this is a super way to get rid of your *chametz* before Pesach."

Zahava got busy with her task and Devoiry returned to the chicken. "Okay, ladies, the best part. Open up a cartoon of Tofutti sour cream — what would we do without pareve sour cream, I ask you? Slide it into the chicken dish and keep stirring till it's all dissolved. Got that, Suze?"

"Got it," she said, as she stirred.

"Looks delicious. So easy!" commented a woman in the front row.

"Of course it's easy. You might assume that delicious, gourmet, unique dishes are difficult or time consuming, but I'm as busy as you are raising a family, and if it isn't easy, it's not on my menu. So, speaking of easy, let's move on to the last item on our menu, and then we can all eat and enjoy."

Hope the experiment worked. I'm so scared I could faint.

Devoiry brought out a humongous salad bowl where she had placed all of the salad greens she had washed and prepared before coming.

"I said that my recipes aren't time consuming. Don't talk to me about how much time it takes these days to prepare salad greens to be sure they're bug free! But we love a good salad, don't we ladies, so I did all that prep work at home. It's worth it! Let me show you the easiest salad dressing you'll ever make. It'll save you tons of money, too — no need anymore to buy bottled salad dressing week after week.

Thanks, Yossi, for encouraging me to save money on bottled salad dressing. This dressing's always a hit.

Devoiry sliced a lemon in half and squeezed it with a glass citrus squeezer whose sole purpose was to wring out every last drop of juice from a lemon. "When you're done, just pour the lemon juice directly on the salad, leaving the seeds behind. Now, add a splash of olive oil, sprinkle on a whole lot of dried basil, and garlic salt to taste, and, voilà, that's it!" Devoiry tossed the dressing throughout the salad. "Ready to serve. How long did that take me — about thirty seconds?"

"Why do you put salt into your salad dressing?" asked Zahava, who was placing the last clump of chocolate candy on the tray. "Aren't we all watching our sodium? Can't you use a Mrs. Dash salt-free alternative instead?"

You really are uptight about healthy eating, aren't you? Mr. Weiss loves his chopped liver; that'll make you nuts.

"I happen to live with a bunch of salt lovers, but, of course, you can take these recipes home and substitute whatever works best for you. Speaking of substitutes, I'm going to take this fork," she said, grabbing one she had ready, "and sample the chicken stroganoff. Drum roll, please... The debut of this recipe, and I did it for the Lancaster sisterhood!"

Please G-d, may it be delicious.

Devoiry opened the lid and stabbed a small piece of cooked chicken with her fork. She blew on the chicken, recited a *shehakol* out loud to a chorus of amens, and placed it in her mouth, closing her eyes to best experience the flavor.

The room went silent. She opened her eyes.

And smiled.

"Ladies, *gam zu l'tovah* that my beef went walkin' — I'll never, *bli neder,* make beef stroganoff again. Wait till you taste it!"

Out with the gourmet fancy beef, in with the heimish chicken. Whew, that was close.

She picked up the tray of chocolates and walked over to the freezer in the kitchen. She felt like kicking off her heels and shouting a big yeah!

"Now, while we're enjoying the meal, we'll put these candies in the freezer. By the time we're ready for dessert, we'll have a yummy chocolate treat awaiting us," she said.

She turned to Zahava and handed her a kitchen

wipe. "Thanks, partner. Great job! And thanks to Susie as well. The chicken stroganoff is going to be served with a mushroom brown rice that I made before you all got here and that's been warming in the oven. You've got the recipe for that as well in your packet.

"Everyone give my *sous chefs* a round of applause, and then go out to the social hall and find your plates, bring 'em into the kitchen, and let's get you served up. If you want to make *hamotzi,* there are washing sinks in the social hall and bread on the table, compliments of our local bakery, Lachmeinu."

"And one more thing — if anyone would like to purchase my new cookbook, I'm reducing the cost by five dollars off retail, so if you buy it today, it's only $25. Come see me if you're interested. I'll even throw in a free autograph."

Please G-d, let me go home with an empty box!

"Are these recipes from today in there?" asked one of the women.

"No, they're in your packet, but my new chicken stroganoff recipe will be in the next cookbook — if you all like it, of course. Let me know."

Devoiry breathed deeply as she watched the ladies file out. *That was a close one. Gotta find that beef. Yossi won't appreciate losing five pounds of meat.*

"Excuse me, Devoiry, may I ask you something?" Zahava was standing next to her, empty plate in hand, waiting to be served.

"Of course." *You want the calorie count, too?*

Devoiry spooned out the chicken stroganoff onto Zahava's plate with a side of rice and salad.

"I was wondering...if, you know, well, can I speak to you privately for just a sec?"

"Ah, sure. Suze? Do me a favor and dish out the meal? I'll be just a moment."

Susie stepped out of line and took the ladle from Devoiry's hand. "No problem. Take your time."

Devoiry stepped to the corner of the kitchen, away from the crowd, and Zahava followed.

"Okay, fire away. What'dya want to know?"

Zahava's hands, holding her plate, trembled slightly, and she took one hand and brushed her brunette bangs off her forehead. "I wanted to speak to you about Mr. Weiss," she said. "He and I have a date this evening. Mrs. Weiner just wouldn't leave him alone, kept calling him and pestering him. I guess he caved in just to get her off his back! We talked briefly and agreed to meet tonight."

"Terrific. Mr. Weiss is such a mensch. We've known him for many years. Now I understand why he canceled his usual Tuesday evening dinner with us." *Don't get invested, girl. He'll never go for you. Should I tell you now and spare you the pain?*

Zahava blushed. "I feel so foolish asking this question," she said. "I liked the way he spoke to me on the phone, and I hear good things. For the first time in a long time, I'm intrigued. At my age, you can't imagine the suggestions that are put forward. Mr. Weiss sounds like just the kind of man I've been looking for, but..."

You wanna know if he's a healthy eater? Nope! The more cream sauce, the better.

"But what?"

"When you're in your fifties, looks aren't supposed to matter. It's all about *middos*, right?" Zahava looked pensive.

"Who says that? Anyway, he's quite handsome, very well dressed, like you, and quite —

"Tall? Please tell me he's tall. You see, I'm five feet eleven with no shoes on, over six feet tall with my heels, and I wasn't comfortable asking him his height when we spoke, and my mother didn't know, and I didn't want to get Mrs. Weiner started by asking her directly. I'll be so embarrassed if I show up tonight in these heels and it turns out he's up to my shoulders."

Height is not your problem. Wait till he orders something with two thousand grams of sodium in it.

Devoiry reached her hand up and touched Zahava's shoulder. "Not to worry. No one told you this? Mr. Weiss could dust my ceiling fan without a ladder! He's well over six feet tall."

Zahava's face brightened. "Seriously? Oh, my goodness, you have no idea how relieved I am. *So* many dates, all these years, I walk into the restaurant and the look on his face says it all. He stands up and looks up to me, and I know the date is over before it started. So really, he's tall? *Really* tall?

"Like a giraffe tall. Do you know what he once told me? His nickname in high school was leaf eater!"

Zahava grinned. She suddenly looked ten years younger, early forties at the most. "Now I can put on my best heels tonight and not worry!"

"Where are you going to eat?"

"Mr. Weiss tells me there is a kosher Chinese restaurant less than an hour outside of Lancaster, in Harrisburg."

"Sure, yes. The food is delicious. And, you'll be happy to know, they don't use MSG." *Wish I could see your face when he orders General Tso's Chicken, a heart attack on a plate.* "Enjoy — I look forward to hearing all about it."

"Thanks so much. I can't wait to enjoy your lunch now. Even if it is a ton of calories!"

"Nah, it's not so bad. Brown rice, salad, chicken, veggies — so it has a bit of fat. Live it up!"

Wish I could listen in as you dine over your brown rice and tell Mr. Weiss why everything on his plate is bad for him. Good luck!

Zahava left to join her mother, and Devoiry walked over to the stove to give herself another taste of her new, phenomenal, *gam zu l'tovah* meal, chicken stroganoff.

Joy and gratitude radiated through her as she

heard murmurs of delight pass across the room.

"Isn't this amazing? It's worth the calories!"

"I can't wait to serve this for Shabbos. Won't my husband be surprised."

"This salad dressing is so fresh and tasty!"

"Who knew that beef stroganoff doesn't need beef?"

"That Devoiry Rosenberg, she's so talented. She should really do more catering!"

"I've got to get her cookbook!"

Music to her ears. All she had hoped for, and more. She piled a heaping spoonful of her new creation onto her plate and walked over to join her good friend, Susie.

"Hey, Devoiry, you did it again. Home run! Come sit down." Susie ushered her to a seat at a table full of women Devoiry had known for years.

Good. They all look like they're enjoying the food.

"Thanks, Suze. I appreciate it. What kind of lunatic wears heels to a cooking demo? Great to get off my feet!" She pulled up a chair next to Susie, and once seated, slipped her heels off to give her feet room to breathe.

"Love the salad dressing. I'll be making it at home," said Carol, her longtime neighbor.

"Spread the word. Share the recipe with your friends," said Devoiry. "And don't forget, I have a cookbook for sale." *Put her enthusiasm to work!*

"So, where did the meat go? Any ideas?" asked

Nora, an old friend and mother of Chava, Bracha's best friend for over three years.

Devoiry's stomach lurched. "Thanks for reminding me. I was just enjoying my lunch. I'd better find that meat or Yossi will never let me hear the end of it!"

Twelve

THE DAY AFTER HER COOKING demo, Devoiry was looking forward to the part of preparing new recipes she enjoyed the most — shopping for ingredients and dreaming up fresh ideas.

"Hey Dev, I've been waiting for a moment to show you something when the kids are in school," Yossi said, thrusting a large black canvas bag onto the dining room table.

Devoiry already had her coat on, purse in hand. They were driving down to Baltimore together so she could shop at Trader Joe's in Pikesville while he visited his new client, Mr. Teitelbaum. Yossi insisted on being on time for his 10 a.m. appointment and she wasn't going to be the reason for his getting there late. But if his agenda was the reason for the delay, why not? She backtracked to the dining room.

"Let me guess. You found something on sale, and even though it's January, you're putting it away for Chanukah?" she teased.

He grinned. "Better than that," he said. "Wedding presents!"

Devoiry cocked her head. "Wedding? We're invited to a wedding I don't know about?" She walked closer to the table to inspect the bag. *It's big and heavy, whatever it is.*

"Nope. These are for *our* kids when they get married. Look, I'll show you."

"Excuse me? Have we joined a new religion that believes in child brides?" she joked. "May I remind you that our daughters are eleven and fourteen? What have you done?"

Yossi removed from the bulky bag four framed pictures, heavily wrapped in thick plastic.

"Let me show you, Dev. These are amazing! Remember a few months ago the shul brought this Israeli artist into town who specializes in color micrography?"

"You bought these there?"

"No. We were tied up that day, but I got to thinking. The artist was offering a special — buy three, get the fourth free — and her work is really expensive, and we have four kids. So I thought, why not invest now, buy each kid his own micrography, and then give it to each of them as a wedding present when we get them to the *chuppah?*"

Tully is eight years old, and you just bought him a wedding present because you could save money? Please tell me you're kidding!"

"Oh, but it gets even better! I secured a coupon for Michaels arts and crafts store — 60 percent off your total custom framing order. I got in touch with the artist before she came to town, and she sent me her info. I saw all of the prints she had available for sale, and I picked out a different one for each of our kids, according to their personalities. I left a check by the person running the event and she held the prints for me."

Yossi was breathless with excitement. "Then, using my Michaels coupon, I had each one custom framed! Look, you have to see these. They're amazing! I've been hiding them in my car and waiting to show you."

Devoiry couldn't stop shaking her head. *Whoever heard of buying your kids a wedding present ten years before the chuppah?*

Devoiry plopped herself down on a dining room chair. "Let the art show begin," she muttered. *Just don't blame me for being late!*

Yossi gingerly took the first framed art off the pile and showed it to Devoiry. "For Mordy, a drawing of tefillin, made up of the *tefillos* that are inside."

"Stunning, and I love the mahogany frame." She peered closely at the tiny Hebrew letters strung together to form a realistic picture of tefillin. "Mordy will *love* this! And for Bracha?"

He slid off the pile a large, ornate gold frame with a picture of a delicate red rose, made up entirely from the words of *Shir HaShirim*. "For our lovely rose, who continues to blossom, even if sometimes she's a bit thorny to live with!" He laughed.

"Next," he said, bringing out a second, smaller, bright blue frame with a vivid, colorful scene of *kriyas Yam Suf*, constructed from the entire *sefer Shemos*. The scene was dizzying, thousands of miniscule Hebrew words artfully arranged to make up an intricate design. "This is for our Malka, because she's our most colorful character, and getting her to the *chuppah* could be like parting the Yam Suf!"

"Oh, Yossi, stop it. She's as much a catch for some *yeshivah bachur* as Bracha is! Can't wait to see what you picked out for Tully! Matchbox cars?"

He tilted the last frame upright. It was a rustic, copper-framed picture of the Kosel, calligraphied out of the entire *sefer Tehillim*. Devoiry just sat still, drinking it all in. "Yossi, I can't get over this... can you imagine the patience it takes to do one of these? She's really quite a talent. You got me this time, Yoss...I'm speechless!"

"I love them, too. We'll put them away in a

good, safe spot, and each kid will get his on the day of his *chasunah*!"

Devoiry's eyes brimmed with tears.

"What'sa matter? You mad at me or something?" he asked. "I saved a bundle!"

Devoiry stood and heaved her large purse back on her shoulders. "Yossi, you never cease to amaze me. The way you nailed each picture, just right for each child. It's really cool. I could actually see each of them receiving these on their big day. Makes me realize that the nest will be emptying sooner than I'm ready!"

She wiped the trickle of tears from her cheeks. *No time for this today; we have an appointment to make.* "So, what didya pick out for me?" she teased to lighten the mood.

"I was going to buy you one the artist created for *Eishes chayil,* but I was already over budget. You're my *eishes chayil* for sure — don't need a picture to remind me! Now, we have to get going so we aren't late. Be right back."

"I'll wait in the car for you. Just lock up." Devoiry was struck by a tender feeling for her husband. *He tries so hard to be a good father. We should appreciate him more.*

"Oh, Yoss, by the way, I've noticed that Malka's tics have been so much better in the last few days. Since our meeting at the school, you've been much lighter around the house. I think it's making a real difference for her. Thanks."

Yossi lifted the framed pictures into his arms and headed for the stairs to the finished attic. "Trying, Dev, trying. Sometimes I just have to learn to keep my mouth shut. I'll be right out. You can warm up the car meanwhile."

After a seventy-five-minute drive of companionable conversation, Yossi dropped Devoiry off at the Pikesville Trader Joe's, where she had a full ninety minutes to shop, while Yossi met with Mr. Teitelbaum. She was always on the lookout for new kosher items on Trader Joe's shelves, and she'd have plenty of time to put together new recipe ideas as she shopped. And those pareve chocolate chips? She'd buy twenty bags if they had plenty in stock. Nothing better than Trader Joe's chocolate chips.

Devoiry pulled a shopping cart out of the lineup, and reviewed in her mind the upcoming catering job and the items needed. She opened her purse to pull out her list, knowing that she'd come home with triple what was on the list anyway. She eagerly headed to her first stop, the dry pasta aisle. *I'll need at least four pounds of the brown-rice pasta for that family who requested a gluten-free pasta salad for certain family members with celiac.*

Devoiry selected the brown-rice spaghetti she usually purchased. She lifted it to check for the *hechsher,* just to be sure it hadn't changed since the last shopping trip.

"Devoiry, is that you?"

She whirled around at the sound of a familiar voice, and then looked up. "Zahava? How are you? That's right, you live down here, don't you!" Wow, in my flats, I feel like a midget next to you."

Zahava laughed. "Actually, my friends accuse me of living at Trader Joe's! No preservatives, no artificial ingredients. I'm in Gan Eden here. I shop here every day, live right down the street. That pasta you're holding," Zahava reached out and took it from her hand and held it up to look at it, "you buy that one often?"

Oh, don't tell me. It has something you don't approve of in it?

"Whenever I get down here I pick some up, yes." Devoiry threw several more brown rice packages into her cart. *That'll show you.*

"Do you mind if I show you a pasta that tastes even better, without any wheat?"

Yes, I do.

Devoiry shrugged. "I've always been happy with this one."

"It's not bad, but try this one instead." She pulled out a buckwheat pasta Devoiry had never seen before. "New to the market. I'm here every day, so I notice when something new hits the shelf. I just tried it last week. Phenomenal! You can consider me your personal shopper!"

Except you'll only recommend bland and boring.

"Great. Thanks!" Devoiry placed one package in the cart, noting to herself that when Zahava had moved on, she needed to put three more packages of the familiar brown-rice pasta in the cart.

"So Zahava, wasn't last night your date with Mr. Weiss?" Devoiry tried to look nonchalant. Zahava's face shifted to somber in seconds.

"Yes, we met in Harrisburg, and then I drove back home late last night. You recommended that restaurant? Oy, everything was swimming in oil and salt. I can't understand —

I don't care what you ate. I want the scoop.

"So do you think you and Mr. Weiss will get together again?"

"I doubt it. First he ordered fried wantons, then this horrible chicken dish, General something or other. I could barely stand looking at him eat it."

Zahava played with the button on her sleeve, fingering it as if she was testing it to be sure it was secure.

Devoiry reached over to a shelf to grab a few bags of a couscous and lentil mix she often served for Shabbos, and she threw them into the cart.

"Zahava, I could have told you — Mr. Weiss likes food, lots of it, and the saltier the better."

Devoiry started placing into her cart can after can of her favorite low-fat marinara sauce, which she always stocked up on at Trader Joe's. Zahava reached out for a couple of cans herself and placed them into her cart. "Good selection. I love this sauce, and no extra sugar!"

Devoiry straightened up from bending down to get the cans. "I'm glad we agree!"

Zahava sighed. "I wish I knew what to do. I'm so confused."

"About tomato sauce?"

"No. About Jacob. I haven't met a man as nice as him in years, and to find someone who loves to travel as much as I do? It seems too good to pass up. He's even tall enough for me. If I could just get past what he puts on his plate!"

I wonder if Mr. Weiss is interested in her. Should I encourage her?

"Zahava, walk with me while I visit my favorite aisle — the one with those pareve chocolate chips. Bet you don't eat them, right?" she teased.

Zahava blushed. "You caught me. My only vice. I let myself have ten chocolate chips a day!"

Hashem, help me. Is she for real?

Devoiry aimed her cart toward the large pile of chocolate chips heaped at the end of the aisle. "Listen, I've known Mr. Weiss for many years, and he's a diamond. Not a diamond in the rough, the newlywed kind that has lots of potential but needs plenty of training. This one's already been polished. If I were standing in your shoes..."

Devoiry picked up a package of chocolate chips and tossed them in Zahava's direction. They caught Zahava by surprise and bounced off her neatly tucked in, button-down Oxford shirt before she caught them, and then she flinched when she saw the crease it made.

"If I were you," Devoiry continued, "I'd practice eating twenty chocolate chips a day, and work your way up to living dangerously. And then, I'd give Mrs. Weiner a call and suggest a second date with Mr. Weiss."

Thirteen

DEVOIRY FINISHED UP HER TRADER Joe's shopping and joined up with Yossi at the appointed time when he pulled up in front of the store, as punctual as he always was. She took one look at his face and knew they'd be celebrating soon. He jumped out of the car to help her load her groceries with the energetic step of a nineteen-year-old boy.

"About $2,500 a month, that's what I can save him, and that's just for starters. Quick review, I bet I can do even better!" He lifted two bags at a time and hefted them into the trunk.

"Terrific, Yoss. I'm so happy for you. When do we get a complimentary dinner again?" she asked as she slid into the front seat, letting him take over the bag shlepping.

"Patience, my dear. Patience!" he shouted to her as he finished loading the car, and then walked the cart to its resting place.

"How was your shopping?" he asked. "Any good bargains?"

"No worries, good prices, and some new recipe ideas already churning in my head. And you'll never believe who I ran into!"

"Zahava."

"How'd you guess?"

"Because Jacob called me on my cell after I dropped you off, before I got to my meeting. So I knew she was back home. Health nut, lives in Baltimore, Trader Joe's, it's not a stretch."

"What did he say about their date?" she asked.

Yossi shrugged. "Nothin' much. Very intelligent, he was amazed to find someone who loves to travel as much as he does, but he said it'll never work, no sense going on a second date."

Devoiry's stomach lurched. "You didn't agree with him, did you?"

Yossi turned his head toward Devoiry. "Since when do you think this *shidduch* is a good idea? Of course I told him to forget about it. He said he could never live with her, because she kept eyeing his plate like he was eating sticks of dynamite or something. You know Jacob — he likes his food. The more salt the better. Your bubby's potato kugel isn't exactly health food. He said he felt like she was inspecting everything he ordered like she was his doctor or something. Who needs that in a wife?" Yossi stopped at a light and turned on the CD player. "So I told him he was right, forget about her."

"And I told Zahava that she should call Mrs. Weiner and ask for a second date!" Devoiry cried.

Avraham Fried came blasting out of the CD player at a decibel level ten times higher than planned. Devoiry reached for the knob to lower the music so they could continue their conversation.

"Yossi, I'm not so sure this *shidduch* is a disaster. Sure, they've got some issues to work out. But this Zahava, I think she's really lonely. Maybe she could bend a bit?"

"She'd better, or she's going to be eating those sprouts of hers alone," Yossi said.

Fourteen

DEVOIRY CRACKED EIGHT EGGS, ONE at a time, into the glass bowl, checked them, and then slid them into her KitchenAid, beating them with her wire whip attachment at speed 6 until they were frothy and double in size. A full pound of Trader Joe's chocolate chips, one-fourth of a cup of strong coffee, and two sticks of margarine were melting in her double boiler. Although the recipe called for butter, in deference to a *fleishig* Shabbos, she'd learned that margarine worked almost as well.

"Sorry, Zahava. I know you'll hate the idea of all this margarine," she said aloud.

Zahava and Jacob were coming for Shabbos lunch the following day, and Devoiry couldn't remember when she'd been so nervous. Suddenly all of her bubby's recipes were suspect — too much salt, fat, cholesterol. *I bought bison meat, lower cholesterol, for the cholent instead of flanken — hope no one can tell the difference. Should I make a broccoli kugel instead of potato? No one ever eats it after the first bite. At least Zahava could eat the salmon for an appetizer, right? Unless she doesn't eat the soy sauce I put on it because it's too salty.*

"Zahava, girl, you're driving *me* nuts. How's Jacob ever going to live with you?" she muttered.

Devoiry inspected her melted chocolate and margarine concoction and turned the flame off. She tested the mixture with her instant-read thermometer: 115 degrees. Perfect. She stirred it a few times, inhaling the scrumptious aroma of melted chocolate. She kissed her fingertips and touched one of her favorite magnets: "I would give up chocolate, but I'm not a quitter." Life without a steady diet of chocolate was just unimaginable.

She prepared her water bath, blended the chocolate mixture with the frothy eggs, one-third at a time, until she had a glorious bowlful of shiny, warm chocolate, which she then lightly turned into her nine-inch springform pan prepared with parchment paper on the bottom and aluminum up the sides to prevent water seeping in while baking. She placed the pan into a 325-degree oven, set the timer for eighteen minutes, and then came her favorite part. She glanced furtively around the kitchen, even though she knew she was alone, with Mordy upstairs studying for midterms, and then took that same spatula and scraped the bowl to scoop up the chocolate still clinging to its sides.

"Mmm...mmm!" she said, licking her lips. "Yossi, you'd be proud of me. I didn't waste a bit!"

"Hi, Ima!" Devoiry startled, caught in the act.

Mordy bounded into the kitchen and went to the fridge to get himself some soda.

"Ah, hi, Mordy. Done studying?" Devoiry wiped her mouth with a napkin, hoping there wasn't chocolate all over her lips.

"Nope, not done. Just need a break. This history midterm is going to be a bear. Too much memorizing of facts I could care less about. Like, when am I ever going to really need to know about the Han Dynasty in China and its twenty-eight accomplishments?

"Understood. I feel your pain. Speaking of accomplishments, I'm really proud of the way you rewrote that history paper. Maybe the one you wrote on your own got a B, not an A, but in my book, your efforts to get that B are much more appreciated than any A you got using Shmueli's work."

Mordy reached his long index finger into the KitchenAid bowl and lifted his chocolate-filled finger to his mouth.

"Mmm, Ima, you get an A for chocolate. Can't

wait to eat the mousse when it's finished!"

Devoiry glanced sideways at Zahava, who was sitting to her left, and tried to camouflage her intense need to know what she was putting into her mouth. *Good, she's eating the salad. I only put my homemade olive oil and lemon dressing on it. And she seems to be enjoying the cholent and the broccoli kugel. She's not touching the potato kugel, no surprise.* Devoiry was so tense from watching Zahava's plate and what was or was not on it that she could scarcely enjoy her own food.

"Devoiry, your cholent is delicious," she said as she polished off a biteful of the bison meat that Devoiry had made plentiful in the cholent. "I'm not normally much of a meat eater, but I could look forward to this every Shabbos!"

"Thank you. I'm glad you're enjoying it." *If you only knew how hard I tried to put together a meal you'd eat.*

Tully was off playing, and the girls were at a school Shabbaton. Mordy was eating by a friend, so it was just the four of them at the table. Jacob was sitting next to Yossi, and while they were conversing about the weekly parashah, Devoiry took advantage of the opportunity to get to know Zahava a bit better. She had noticed when Zahava and Jacob walked through the door that they had a comfortable energy together, that they had become accustomed to one another in just a short time. This was really going somewhere.

"Can I ask you something, Zahava?"

"Sure."

Devoiry wrestled with a momentary pang of jealousy as she took in Zahava's pressed linen suit, perfectly manicured fingernails, and diamond pendant. *I feel like a shlump next to her. She's older than me, but you'd never know it.*

"When did you develop such a...ah...mission to eat healthy? Is it something you've felt strongly about all your life?"

Please tell me there was a time you were normal.

"Are you kidding me? I used to be fifty pounds heavier, and chocolate was my best friend. I was addicted to my morning mocha latte. And potato kugel? Forget about it. Every Shabbos, I'd put out a tray for the guests, and then eat whatever hadn't been finished off before *shalosh seudos!*"

Now we're talkin'. She's cool.

"So what happened?"

Zahava's mouth twitched as darkness flitted across her face. "Cancer. My late husband. We tried everything. Nothing worked. Not the davening, the chemo, the diet. But" — her face brightened considerably — "I couldn't get over how much better I felt after getting myself off the sugar/chocolate/carbs treadmill. I did the cancer diet with him, just so he wouldn't have to do it alone, and after he was *niftar*, I kept following the diet." Zahava stared out into space, lost in memories. "First, I guess, just because it made me feel closer to him. But then, as the years went by, I never went back to my old ways because I felt so much better."

Maybe I should try this diet. But it sure doesn't jive with being a gourmet chef.

Zahava stared at Devoiry. "I hope I don't make you uncomfortable. It's not for everyone, this diet I stick to. I don't mean to insinuate that, well, that everyone should do it. It just works so well for me."

Zahava leaned over and whispered to Devoiry, "Do you think Jacob is a hopeless cause? I'm not going to get him to give up salt and sugar, am I?"

She sat back up in her chair and glanced over at Jacob, who was so immersed in a *devar Torah* with Yossi that it was as if no one else was in the room. Devoiry watched a smile form on Zahava's lips and her eyes brighten when she looked in his direction.

She likes him.

"You figured that out, huh?" asked Devoiry. "Yeah, I'd say that's unlikely. Maybe over time, but I don't think he's going to convert to bean sprouts and tofu anytime soon."

Jacob looked up from his conversation with Yossi and his eyes rested on Devoiry and Zahava. "What are you girls chatting about? You plotting something about me?"

"We're trying to figure out how to make Bubby's potato kugel out of Jerusalem artichokes and cauliflower," bantered Zahava. "Devoiry has some great ideas!"

"*No*, you can't touch Bubby's kugel. It's off-limits! But don't worry, I'll eat some salad." He reached out for the salad bowl and scooped himself up a pile of leafy greens.

"Devoiry, if I start going through potato and salt withdrawal, can I come here and replenish my reserves?"

"You're always welcome, Jacob." Devoiry turned toward Zahava and smiled. "And so are you. I'll keep a supply of carrot sticks on hand for you."

Devoiry stood and lifted up her plate to clear, with Zahava's as well. "Can I interest you in a sliver of flourless chocolate torte, or have you already reached your chocolate quota for today?" she teased.

Zahava stood to help Devoiry clear the table. "Let's celebrate our new friendship. I'd be delighted to sample your torte. I'm sure it's delicious."

"Jacob, there's hope!" Devoiry called out as she walked to the kitchen. "But if you get desperate, you can always come here to carbo-load!"

Devoiry and Zahava worked on clearing the table and preparing the dessert while the men talked companionably. Suddenly the door opened and Bracha breezed in unexpectedly with two of her friends in tow.

"Ima, the food at the Shabbaton is gross! We walked home from the house we're staying at to see if you've got anything better for us to eat. We're starving!"

Devoiry stepped away from the counter and walked toward the girls. "You didn't insult your host, did you? *Chas v'shalom!* I'm sure she tried very hard to give you something yummy."

Bracha rolled her eyes. "Ima, we're not that stupid. We told her everything was amazing, and wonderful, and stupendous. But it wasn't! We told her I had to pick up something I forgot. Can you feed us now, pleeeeeease? If I have to eat one more bite of that, what she called, kugel thing, I think I'll —

"Enough, okay, got the picture. Nice to see all of you anyway," Devoiry said, glancing at Bracha's friends, who were taking their coats off and hanging them on the hooks by the front door. "Do you want more main-course food? We're having dessert now. But I can bring back some of the main meal."

"Mrs. Rosenberg, do you have any kugel left? I love your kugel!" said Bracha's friend Chani.

"Sure. Of course. Tell ya what, girls. Why don't you seat yourselves at the kitchen island and I'll bring out for you what we had for lunch. But only if you'll never mention this to your host!"

Bracha swiped her thumb and index finger over her lips. "Lips sealed. Thanks, Ima. You saved us!"

Devoiry busied herself with feeding the girls and encouraged Zahava to make herself comfortable back at the table. When she returned with dessert in hand for Yossi, Jacob, and Zahava, she found Zahava and Yossi in a heated discussion about Yossi's favorite topic.

"That organic food you eat all the time, I can't get over how expensive it is!" Yossi complained. "Do you really think it's worth all that added cost? To me, an apple is an apple is an apple. What do I need with this no-pesticides, grown-only-in-the-purest-of-soil, never-been-waxed kind of thing that they get to charge twice as much for?"

Jacob moved to defend Zahava. "You know, Yossi, it's not always about the money."

You tell him. He doesn't listen to me.

"What I mean is, Zahava tells me that the simple apple we find in the grocery isn't the apple Hashem blessed us with, but some replication of an apple that has been poisoned with all kinds of chemicals."

Yossi leaned back in his chair and whistled. "She got to you, man. What happened to my old friend, Jacob, who would eat whatever was put in front of him with gusto? You're not turning into one of those bean sprout hippies, are you?"

Zahava and Jacob laughed and shared a glance between them. "Don't worry, Yossi," said Zahava. "The old Jacob you've known and loved all these years is still very much there. But I did convince him to start eating organic apples, so that's a start anyway."

Wonder how much Jacob will change to make a life with Zahava. Remains to be seen. I don't think he'll ever give up his potato kugel.

Devoiry took a spoonful of her luscious chocolate torte and relished the fact that somewhere, someone once said, "Shabbos calories don't count." She chose to believe that, indeed, this must be true.

Fifteen

Devoiry patiently waited on the deli line at the local Glatt Mart, repeatedly glancing at her reliable Timex watch, even though she already knew the time — 9:40 a.m. She needed to get back before Jessica showed up to help her in the kitchen. Finally reaching the counter, she placed her order for four pounds of assorted cold cuts, which, when transformed, would become the ubiquitous deli rolls that her customers always requested.

"Thanks a lot, Sam," she said as she took the cold cuts from the harried meat counter helper and went to stand in line at the register to pay. *It's 9:46. Oh, gosh, I cut it too close. Hope Jessica's running late. What if she leaves?*

"'Mornin' Mrs. Rosenberg. Lotta meat today.

'Nother cook demo?" asked the register employee, a sweet Israeli girl who had learned enough English to get by. "No, Efrat, just a catering job, and this time, I'm not leaving my meat at the register!"

"Yes, missus. I feel so bad when you did that. Ran to the lot, but you was gone."

Devoiry lifted her grocery bag in her hand. "Got it this time, Efrat. I'm not making that mistake again!" She rushed out the door, glancing at her watch again. *Yikes, 9:53!*

Just then, she saw Mrs. Weiner waving from across the parking lot. "Devoiry, we've got to talk!"

Oh, goodness. No time for her right now.

"Hi, Mrs. Weiner... I'm rushing. We'll talk later!" she called out as she got into her car. She glanced at the dashboard clock. 9:56. *Gotta scram. Please, Jessica, don't leave!*

She drove the two miles to her home far over the speed limit, alternating her prayers between "Please don't give me a ticket," and "Please be waiting for me, Jessica." She was relieved when she pulled into her street and saw Jessica's light blue Honda parked by the house. *Baruch Hashem.* Made it!

She pulled in the driveway and bounced out of the car, breathless. Jessica got out of her car and walked to meet her at the front door.

Wow, she looks amazing in that skirt. So tznius.

"Sorry to keep you waiting! Been waiting long?" Devoiry asked.

"Just a few minutes, no problem. I figured you got tied up somewhere. Look!"

Jessica pointed at a long jean skirt that looked crisp, new, and quite lovely. "I bought this for you! Didn't want to give your food any bad energy today!"

"You look marvelous. I'm so glad you came, and of course you would have been most welcome in your old jeans, too! Please come in. Excuse the mess. How I'm going to get this place cleaned up for Shabbos, I have no idea!"

Devoiry opened the front door and hung their winter coats in the closet. She kicked off her winter shoes and replaced them with her well-worn sheepskin slippers. "Want to borrow Bracha's slippers for the day?" she offered.

"Nah, I'm fine, but thanks. So, what are we making today?" she asked as they walked into the kitchen.

"First thing this morning, chocolate chip banana mini muffins, then I've got the deli meat here in my hand for deli rolls, and that's just for starters. Hope you had your coffee this morning!"

Jessica smiled. "I'm a college student, remember? Coffee mornin', noon, and night!"

Devoiry selected a blue-jeans apron with a pocket and placed it over Jessica's head, lifting up Jessica's long brown hair and handing her an elastic to pull it back.

Jessica poked her nose inside the large

KitchenAid permanently parked on the kitchen island. "Ewww, rotten bananas?" she asked, spotting a pile of dark brown bananas resting in the bowl.

"My secret for easy banana bread. Put overripe bananas into the freezer, and then when you're ready to make banana bread, watch how easy this is." Devoiry picked up a kitchen knife and slid the sharp edge of the knife down each banana skin, oozing out the gooey insides into the bowl. "Much easier to mash the bananas when they're frozen and then defrosted."

Devoiry tied a flowered apron around her back that had Scrumptious scrawled across the front, and picked up an index card off the counter.

"So, let's get started. Here's my recipe. I've got all the ingredients already laid out on the counter. All you need to do is dump them into the KichenAid. Just remember, we're doubling the recipe so we have plenty. Here you go."

Jessica picked up the index card marked Chocolate Chip Banana Muffins and read:

4 mashed, overripe bananas	1 teaspoon cinnamon
1 cup all-purpose white flour	3 tablespoons canola oil or
½ cup brown sugar, packed	applesauce
½ cup wheat flour	pinch of salt
⅓ cup strong brewed coffee	1 pinch baking soda
½ cup rolled oats	1 teaspoon vanilla extract
2 large eggs	½ bag Trader Joe's chocolate
1½ teaspoons baking powder	chips

"Just put them into the mixer in any order?" Jessica asked.

"Pretty much. Here's a glass bowl you can use for dissolving the sugar into the coffee before you add it, and here's another glass bowl we'll use for checking the eggs before we drop them in. I'm going to start assembling the deli rolls while you work. Mind if I put on some music?"

"I'm guessing you don't listen to rock and roll," teased Jessica.

"I'll put on something up tempo for us," she said as she plugged her MP3 player into the speakers set up on the kitchen counter, pressed "play," and listened as her favorite medley of Jewish music started up. "I've been known to dance in my kitchen while I'm cooking — but usually when I'm alone! Ever been to an Orthodox wedding?"

Jessica shook her head.

"Well, *im yirtzeh Hashem*," Devoiry said, "we'll be planning one soon for Mr. Weiss and we'll make sure you get an invite. Wait till you see how *frum* Jews celebrate a *simchah*!"

Jessica carefully measured out the ingredients, one at a time. "Mr. Weiss, the man I met over Shabbos? He's getting married?"

Devoiry removed the partially defrosted puff pastry sheets to begin deli roll assembly. "Good possibility, although I really can't believe it myself.

He's been dating a woman, Zahava, for almost two weeks, and —"

"Two weeks?" she exclaimed. "And they're getting married? I dated Chris for two years, and I was never sure whether we should get married!" She dropped the dissolved brown sugar and coffee into the bowl.

Devoiry opened up all of the plastic wrapped cold cuts from Glatt Mart. "You're familiar with the term *bashert*?"

Jessica placed the flour and oats into the bowl. "You mean soul mate, right? Like, two halves of the same whole, meant to be together, all that romantic stuff?"

"Yes, like Yossi and me. Get on each other's nerves sometimes, but we complete each other, too." Devoiry started placing strips of assorted deli meat on the puff pastry, then smeared on mustard and mayo before rolling the pastry up into a roll.

"I love your deli roll, Mrs. Rosenberg. I didn't know it was this easy!" Jessica said as she watched Devoiry take a deli roll from assembly to completion in about ninety seconds.

Devoiry put her finger to her lips. "Shhh. Five minutes prep, happy customers. My kind of recipe."

"You're not seeing Chris anymore, right?" Devoiry asked, trying to sound nonchalant.

"Nope. He graduated last year and moved away

when he got a good job in Boston. We said we'd keep it going, but it all kinda fell apart." Jessica's face looked wistful. "I guess that's best. I was never sure about him anyway."

Devoiry reached for the glass dish and the egg carton. "Let me show you how we do the eggs," she said. "You know, Jessica, when it's *bashert*, you do know. Often on the first date, usually by the second or third. It's not surprising that within a week or two, Mr. Weiss and Zahava would know. It's just a feeling, a knowing, beyond romantic. It's deeper than that."

"So that's what you think is happening with Mr. Weiss and Zahava?" Jessica took four eggs out of their carton, holding two in each hand.

Devoiry paused, her hands in midair, and stared into space. "I can't believe it myself. I was so sure they were completely mismatched, not *bashert*, be- wrong! They didn't hit it off on the first date, but they gave it another try, and from what I hear, and what I saw this past Shabbos, it's been going better and better ever since. Mr. Weiss looks great. He really likes her. He just has to get past her being one of those don't-use-aerosol-cans, wears-only-organically-grown-cotton, never-eats-processed-foods kind of woman. I suppose, as long as they never eat together, they should do fine!"

Jessica cracked an egg against the mixing bowl.

"Wait!" Devoiry reached out her hand. "You

can't put the eggs directly into the mixing bowl."

Jessica's brow arched. "One of those kosher rules, like no pork?"

Devoiry took the cracked egg from Jessica and placed a glass bowl underneath it. "First we crack the egg into the bowl and check for blood — before adding it to the mixing bowl. That way, if we spot blood in the egg, we can discard the egg without ruining the whole batter."

Jessica shrugged. "Whatever. So, what happens if you eat blood? I've been eating eggs without checking them for over twenty years; so far, nothin's happened to me!"

Devoiry cracked all four eggs, one at a time, checked them, and then slid them into the bowl. *I'm not a kiruv rabbi. They know how to respond to these objections.*

"Hashem doesn't hold you responsible for what you didn't already know, but —"

Jessica's face looked pinched. "So I'm better off not learning anything. Then I can stay in the dark and not be blamed!" She tapped the baking soda into the measuring spoon so hard that white particles of baking soda scattered all over the counter.

Help me, Hashem. I'm drowning here.

"Don't worry, let's just sponge that up," Devoiry said as she grabbed a sponge and wiped the counter clean. She stalled for time, cleaning up all the wrappers left behind from the now-empty packages of cold cuts and puff pastry. She threw them in the trash, watching Jessica place the canola oil into the mixer.

"Have you ever thought about how the word 'responsible' could also be pronounced 'response-able'?"

Jessica squinted her eyes. "So?"

"I'm thinking, once you're educated as a Jew, you're more able to respond to what Hashem wants of you."

Jessica pursed her lips. "And this is a good thing? Seems easier just to be secular."

Devoiry rinsed her hands from the deli rolls and pulled out the mini muffin trays from the cabinet. She spread the trays out on the counter and turned the mixer on low.

"Jessica, is an easy life your goal?" Jessica raised her eyes and looked at Devoiry, but then looked away again.

Jessica placed the last ingredient, the vanilla extract, into the bowl and stared at the mixer attachment as it swooshed around and around. Devoiry gazed at it, too, wishing that she could read into the mixture exactly what to say to Jessica to help open her mind, just like the gypsies read tea leaves. Jessica finally broke the silence.

"Who doesn't want an easy life? Like when I ace my finals and I didn't even have to study? Or when the parking spot shows up just when I need it? Or getting a high-paying job when I graduate so I don't have to worry about bills? Sure, easy is good!"

Devoiry stopped the mixer and smoothed down the insides with a spatula, removing the ingredients that had stuck to the sides. "Okay, what if everything seems easy, but none of it really matters?"

"Are you saying it has to be hard to matter?"

Devoiry started chewing her lip. "I'm saying that it helps me, if the decisions I make in my life, like what food to eat, and how to prepare it, or what to wear, or what to pray, aren't all coming from me, and my mood of the day. There's something bigger than me that keeps me married to Yossi even when I'm mad at him, teaches me how to speak to my mother with respect, *kibbud av va'em*, even when she annoys me, gives me something to look forward to every Shabbos. What would the week be like with no Shabbos?" Devoiry started sponging the counter down, getting ready for their next food prep. "Yes, I think my life, in many ways, is a lot easier than yours, actually." *Oy, I'm bombing here. She just looks confused. What would Yossi say?*

"Why? I'm just this single college kid, no obligations, can eat what I want, go where I want, do whatever I feel like. No rules — I don't answer to anyone. I have to keep up my grades so my parents don't get upset, but I like school, so that's really not a big deal."

Devoiry stopped the mixer and lifted out the beater so they could begin pouring the batter into the muffin cups. "You call that easy? Sounds like a nightmare to me. All my obligations are the best part of my life," she said firmly.

Devoiry tried to read the emotion in Jessica's eyes. *She's lonely. She needs a partner, like I have with Yossi. This is so hard to do alone.*

"Let's each take a scooper and spoon out the batter into these muffin tins," she directed Jessica, jumping when the doorbell rang. She wiped her hands on a hand towel and shouted, "Coming!"

"Jessica, keep scooping. Be right back."

She opened the door a crack, reluctant to let the cold air in. "Mrs. Weiner? Sorry I couldn't talk at Glatt. I was rushing. Do you want to come in?"

"No dear, I don't want to be a nuisance." She wrapped her coat tightly around herself and shuddered. "It's one of those days, you just want to stay inside! But I just had to tell you, you're never going to believe what I just saw..."

"Mrs. Weiner, please. I can't have you out there shivering. Come in, come in." She took Mrs. Weiner by the arm and helped her step into the foyer.

"I'm not staying, really I'm not," she objected as Devoiry closed the door behind her to keep the cold wind from coming through the glass pane. She pushed her hat off her head and looked up at Devoiry from her hunched-over position.

"Mrs. Weiner, even if you aren't staying, I can't have you freezing on me in the meantime. So, what did you see that has you so excited?"

Mrs. Weiner straightened and her eyes danced. "I was walking down the avenue, just after I saw you at Glatt, and I was walking by Gideon's Jewelers, and I couldn't help peeking in the window, and you'll never guess who I saw in there!"

"*Nu?*"

"Mr. Weiss!" she smiled triumphantly. "He was bent over the counter, looking at something very carefully!"

"Mrs. Weiner, he told me that his Rolex had broken and he was going to get it fixed at Gideon's. Sorry to burst your bubble."

Devoiry noticed Mrs. Weiner's eyes dull briefly, so she quickly changed the subject. "You said in the parking lot that you wanted to talk to me?"

Jessica walked into the foyer. "Oh, hi, Jessica. This is Mrs. Weiner, our neighbor. Mrs. Weiner, Jessica's a college student at F & M. She's helping me cook today."

"Nice to meet you. I finished scooping the muffins, Mrs. Rosenberg," she said.

"Terrific! Mrs. Weiner was just stopping off to give me some potential good news. Sure you don't want to come in?" she asked Mrs. Weiner again.

Please say no.

"No, darling. I see you're busy. But I just have

to tell you. I was talking to Mrs. Fryberger at the beauty parlor early this morning — you know we go together every Thursday, so we look nice for Shabbos and all. We go at 7:30 a.m. — she opens up for us because we can't stand being there when it's so crowded, oh, the smell of all of those permanent chemicals for the old ladies..."

She took a breath from her run-on monologue and set off again. "So, anyway, she tells me this morning, her daughter, Zahava, turns out, she really has developed quite a feeling for this fellow, this Mr. Weiss of yours. This Zahava, she's a very intelligent woman, and this Mr. Weiss of yours is a real conversationalist, someone who thinks traveling to foreign lands is exotic, not just a pain in the neck! So, anyway, they've had several dates, and I don't know how they're going to work out this Baltimore-Lancaster problem, never mind how impossible it seems to put together a grass-eater with a salt-loving carnivore, but I'm telling you, if the *Eibishter* parted the Red Sea, he can bring these two lonely souls together." She took a deep breath and pronounced with a fierce look in her eyes: "I just know that's why Mr. Weiss was at Gideon's this morning! Mark my words, we'll hear the announcement soon!"

"Amen! I hope you're right, Mrs. Weiner. When we saw them together on Shabbos, it did seem like they were connecting well. I never thought I'd see the day when Zahava would devour a slice of chocolate torte."

Mrs. Weiner smiled. "I'm glad she didn't miss your delicious torte, dear. Life is too short! Remember, I told Mr. Weiss I had a feeling in my *kishkes* that he'd be pleased to meet Zahava, and now I have a feeling in these old bones of mine that they will be under the *chuppah* soon. Our phone lines crossing, it was all meant to be!"

Mrs. Weiner turned slowly, steadying herself with her cane, "Well, ladies, get back to your baking. I'm going to go home and make myself a nice hot cup of tea. I haven't been this happy in months! My meddling has finally gone to good use!"

"Mrs. Weiner," Devoiry said, stopping her halfway out the door, "perhaps it's premature to be celebrating? We haven't heard an announcement yet."

Mrs. Weiner looked over her bifocals and jutted her head forward. "My dear, don't take my *simchah* away. I'm going home and making myself a very large cup of steaming hot tea with plenty of sugar and lemon, and I'm going to savor every drop of it and celebrate the possibility that there may be a celebration, and I had something to do with it. Even at my ripe old age, all alone, I'm still useful!"

Mrs. Weiner turned to go and Devoiry gently shut the door behind her. She faced Jessica, who was rearranging her hair into an elastic.

"Jessica, you like the idea of not answering to anyone? I love my obligations. They remind me that I matter to someone. Look at Mrs. Weiner — see what joy it brings her to think that she brought two people together. *May* have brought them together, that is. Seems like I'm beginning to celebrate prematurely myself."

She put her arm around Jessica's shoulders. "Now, let's get those muffins and deli rolls into the oven, and if I haven't completely worn you out, it's time to start on the chicken salad with mandarin oranges in phyllo cups."

"Have I worn you out with all my questions?" Jessica asked as they walked back to the kitchen.

"*Chas v'shulom*! As long as you don't always expect me to have the answers, keep those questions coming."

Sixteen

For the first time all evening, Devoiry had a moment to gaze from a corner of the large rented hall at the plethora of miniature hors d'oeuvres, cakes, cookies, fruit platters, and vegetable dips carefully arranged on multi-tiered servers for easy viewing and reach. Once again, vanity had taken precedence over sanity, and her two-inch spiked heels burned the bottoms of her feet. The size-eight dress she had squeezed her size-ten frame into was taking the breath out of her rib cage. Her *sheitel*, swept into an updo by the local *sheitel macher*, made her look very much the picture of the *kallah*'s mother, even though she was technically only the caterer.

She had put her head on the pillow for maybe

two hours last night, after she had furiously rolled out dough, carved pineapple and cantaloupe, and made sure that there was plenty of chocolate mousse and mini–chocolate éclairs for the expected crowd of two hundred well-wishers dropping in to share a mazel tov with Jacob and his *kallah*, Zahava.

"Mazel tov, mazel tov, mazel tov. Everything looks so lovely, dear. You outdid yourself this time!" exclaimed Mrs. Weiner as she leaned forward to embrace Devoiry. "One more time, and I can die in peace, knowing that I'm going to Gan Eden!"

"Excuse me?"

"The *shidduch*, darling! The Sages say that once a person has brought three couples together under the *chuppah*, the *shadchan* is ensured a place in *Olam Haba*. This is my second *shidduch* — the first have been married for over twenty years — and I'm running out of time for the third!"

"Well, Mrs. Weiner, this is my first time successfully helping to bring about a *shidduch*, and I must say, it's a wonderful feeling. I didn't like it one bit when that little phone mishap invaded our privacy, but it seems Hashem had a bigger plan, and you and I were just —

"Devoiry, I can't believe you!" interrupted Zahava, radiant in her floor-length black lace skirt with a white silk blouse and glamorous shawl. She kissed Devoiry on the cheek and hugged her.

"I knew you were talented with food, but really, I feel like it's my wedding day already. You will cater our wedding, I hope? A springtime *chasunah*, what fun!"

"I already have the menu planned! Tofu vegetarian egg rolls, chickpea chummus, plain salmon with lemon, and a sprig of dill, steamed potatoes, no salt, and of course — chocolate torte for dessert!"

Zahava laughed. "Jacob would never let me get away with it. I'm afraid you'll have free license to bring on all your favorites, and I'll bite my tongue!"

Zahava went to greet other guests, and Devoiry noticed Mrs. Goldstein coming her way. "Devoiry, mazel tov," Mrs. Goldstein said. "They seem very well suited for one another. How nice to see."

"Mazel tov, and thank you so much, Mrs. Goldstein, for all the help you've given our Malka. Have you noticed, her tics have just about disappeared, and she's like a different child. You were so kind to give her special consideration on her tests at school; it made all the difference." Devoiry's eyes welled up. She reached over to hug Mrs. Goldstein, allowing herself to forget for a moment that she was hugging the principal. For that second, they were two mothers who understood one another.

"I'm so glad I could help. That's what gives me real *nachas*, to see bright girls like Malka succeed in reaching their potentials. Speaking of potential, you seem to have exceeded yours today. When, *b'ezras Hashem,* I'm marrying off my children, I'll be calling you, *bli neder,* for their *vorts*!"

"Thanks. It's really not that big a deal. This time, I just decided to go with the stand-by recipes that everyone loves, comfort food, I guess you could call it. Amazing how you can take a simple iced chocolate cake, divide it up into individual fancy cupcake papers, and voilà...fancy shmancy. Really, all it is, is simplicity all dressed up!"

Devoiry noted her friend Sharon waving and then walking over with a bookish-looking young woman with thick red glasses and shoulder-length auburn hair. A relative of Zahava's, maybe?

As she waited for Sharon to reach her, she flashed to early that morning when Yossi had given her a hard time about the money she'd spent on the *vort. After* she had stayed up most of the night doing most of the work herself instead of hiring help. Besides, Jacob was paying for all of it, and she'd stayed on budget, so what really was the problem, anyway? Fortunately, though, now that the guests were raving, and Jacob and Zahava looked so happy, Yossi seemed full of *simchah*.

Sharon came to her side and they hugged. She'd known Sharon since Bracha was in diapers. "Devoiry, mazel tov! I'd like to introduce you to someone. Nechama Rubin, this is my friend, Devoiry Rosenberg, the caterer for tonight. The Rosenbergs are close friends of the *chasan*. Devoiry, Ms. Rubin just happened to be visiting Amish country on assignment for the Jewish magazine she writes for, and in search of a kosher meal. Someone in the community told her this was the place to be tonight. I'll leave you ladies to chat. I want to offer a mazel tov to Zahava."

"Nechama, nice to meet you. Where are you visiting from?" Devoiry greeted her, noting her stunning green eyes behind the red frames.

"Israel, actually," she answered in an American accent. "I'm the editorial director for *Jewish Family* — you've heard of it? I made aliyah a year ago when I was offered the job. I used to live in New Jersey."

Sure I've heard of the magazine, but Yossi never thought it was worth the money. Too many photos, not enough content.

"Lovely to meet you. I have to say, your magazine turns out the most gorgeous photos."

"Thank you. It's our strong suit. I'm here with a photographer taking pictures of the Amish community for a future feature we're doing. Since we Orthodox get compared all the time to the Amish — from the non-Jews who don't understand, of course — why not take a closer look at the community?"

Devoiry waved at Jessica, who waved back from across the room. *I'm so glad she came, and she looks lovely in that skirt. Wonder if she bought a new one again.*

"Nechama, has anyone told you the folktale from the Lancaster community? Word has it that many years ago, a chassidic immigrant took the train out from New York, just after arriving from Europe. He glanced out the window of the train, saw these men with beards and black hats, and got off the train, thinking he'd found a chassidic community. By the time he'd found out differently, the train was long gone — so that's how the Orthodox ended up in Lancaster, Pennsylvania!"

Nechama laughed. "I hadn't heard that story. That's precious. Listen, I've been sampling your delicious food since I got here — as you can imagine, getting a kosher meal when you're traveling isn't always easy, so this is a real treat. I love your food. Everything I've tasted has been delish."

"Thanks, I've been at it a long time. I just published my third cookbook, gourmet kosher cooking. For this *vort,* there was no time to get that involved, I kind of threw it together. It's very simple, really.

"I don't know what your gourmet food tastes like, but if I were you, I'd stick with this. This is what our readers want — down to basics, simple, healthy some of the time — other times not so much — but easy and yum!"

Nechama touched Devoiry's elbow and leaned

forward to say something when Mrs. Weiner, who had been leaning on her cane nearby, inserted herself in the conversation.

"I couldn't help overhearing. Nechama, that's your name?"

"Yes, nice to meet you," she said, reaching out her hand to shake Mrs. Weiner's.

Mrs. Weiner peered at Nechama over her bifocals. She was dressed in a blue silk gown that she had told Devoiry she was buying just for this occasion. "Welcome to Lancaster. My name is Mrs. Weiner. Now, I don't mean to intrude on your fun here, but please listen to me. I've been reading your magazine for umpteen years. Lovely photos, but I get through your magazine in half an hour, and I have nothing but time on my hands, so you need to put more in there to read!"

Devoiry expected Nechama's face to tense up in response to Mrs. Weiner's complaint, but she was surprised to see Nechama look at Mrs. Weiner warmly and respond, "I'm with you 100 percent. That's one of the reasons I'm visiting the States. We're recruiting new writers for our magazine. We appreciate loyal readers like you, and you can feel free to tell me anytime what's on your mind."

She reached into her purse, pulled out a business card, and handed it to Mrs. Weiner, who looked very satisfied that the editor of a magazine wanted to listen to what she had to say.

Wish I could take criticism like that about my food without flinching.

Nechama turned back toward Devoiry. "This leads me to what I was about to say. We've been talking at *Jewish Family* about bringing on a food columnist, a writer who will not only share recipes, but will also field questions from our readers. We have many readers like Mrs. Weiner, and her children and grandchildren, who have grown up with the magazine. They think of us as very accessible, like we're family almost, and we pride ourselves in responding to our readers. Lately, all the rage seems to be recipes and cooking. Is this something you might be interested in?"

Shameless, trying to do business at a vort. Rein it in. Keep calm.

"Of course she'd be interested! Who wouldn't be! That's a terrific idea!" Mrs. Weiner intruded. "Devoiry, you don't want to miss this opportunity. Do you know how many women read *Jewish Family*? Everyone I know!"

I'm a big girl. I can handle this myself.

Devoiry smiled at Nechama. "Sounds like a great opportunity. I'd love to talk with you about this when we can really speak, not in the middle of a *vort*. How long are you in town?" she deferred.

"I leave tomorrow afternoon for Israel. I'll let you get back to your party. May I call you tomorrow morning?"

"Of course." Devoiry took one of Nechama's business cards and wrote on the back of it her phone number and handed it back. "I look forward to hearing from you."

Mrs. Weiner reached up and grabbed another business card out of Nechama's hands. "I need another one of your cards. My friend Mrs. Fryberger has what to tell you as well."

Nechama handed Mrs. Weiner a big handful of her business cards. "Mrs. Weiner, feel free to pass out my cards to any of your friends or family. We'd love to hear from all of you!"

"Will do!"

What a nice young lady. I could work for her. This could be a lot of fun. Wait until Yossi hears about this.

"Mazel tov, mazel tov!" Devoiry's friend Susie came over and squeezed her elbow. "You did it! You married off Mr. Weiss, and put on an amazing spread!"

Nechama moved on as Devoiry hugged Susie. "You're not going to believe this. I think I've just been 'discovered.'"

Susie looked at her quizzically.

"That young lady with the red glasses walking over to the buffet table — she's Nechama Rubin, the editorial director for *Jewish Family*. She wants to talk to me about writing a food column for them!"

"What fun! I'm so happy for you. Well deserved. You work so hard!"

"Thanks, Suze. Know what I'm starting to figure out? The less hard I work, the better it goes. I fixed up Mr. Weiss on so many dates, and nothing worked till Mrs. Weiner listened in on my conversation and the *shidduch* came from her! I slave away in my kitchen trying to turn out all these fancy gourmet recipes, and in the end, what do people want? Potato kugel and chocolate éclairs! Look at the buffet table — the éclairs are moving faster than I can keep up with them, and the lox pinwheels that I slaved over to make look pretty are lying there untouched."

"I'm partial to your éclairs myself. So, what are you going to name your new column?" asked Susie. "Try this out." She spread her hands in the air as if she were imagining the name in lights. "Devoiry's Delectables!"

Devoiry wriggled her nose. "Makes me sound like I'm selling candy. No, I'm thinking more like... how 'bout...'Dishing it up with Devoiry!'"

"Oooh, that's fantastic. Great play on words. You and I both know, besides the recipes, the readers love the stories and the chatting about food."

"We'll see if Nechama calls me tomorrow. Hope so."

Devoiry looked out at the crowd that had assembled to wish Jacob and Zahava well. She spotted Zahava chatting comfortably with Jacob's mother, a robust woman in her eighties, as active as a typical sixty-year-old. *Is that a chocolate éclair I see in Zahava's hand? Yahoo!*

She glanced at Jessica, who was engaged in animated conversation with Nechama. Nechama was laughing in between bites of pareve cheesecake, and Jessica looked more relaxed than she had in a long while. *Nechama would be a good friend for Jessica. Closer in age than me, she doesn't trigger the "get off my back, Mom" reflex.*

Baruch Hashem, future food columnist? Maybe a cookbook with Bubby's simple, down-home recipes.

Devoiry raised her glass and said out loud, "*L'chaim!*"